Bill Webster

THE GIRL WITH A PARROT

Limited Special Edition. No. 23 of 25 Paperbacks

Bill was a Theatre Manager at Epsom Playhouse, as well as a Civil Servant for almost 39 years, serving the most vulnerable children and adults in the High Court, especially the Court of Protection. Taught English Literature by Peter Dale, the Modern Poet, he enjoys painting in oils and drawing in pastels. He is married with two children and three grandchildren (so far).

For Bev, Eliot, Jana and Luka (and the new baby coming), Michelle and Monaie.

Bill Webster

THE GIRL WITH A PARROT

AUSTIN MACAULEY PUBLISHERS™

LONDON · CAMBRIDGE · NEW YORK · SHARJAH

A CIP catalogue record for this title is available from the British Library.

ISBN 9781528942737 (Paperback)
ISBN 9781528971263 (ePub e-book)

www.austinmacauley.com

First Published (2019)
Austin Macauley Publishers Ltd
25 Canada Square
Canary Wharf
London
E14 5LQ

Mr Peter Dale, Mr Holmwood and Mr Dick Stoker who taught me English Language and English Literature at Glastonbury.

Chapter 1
We're all at Sea

We are all sitting on the bank of the River Bede, which lies south of Sloping Meadow when Pete, my older brother, comes rushing up to let us know,

"Now it **really** is summer, officially, because we have no more school!"

"Tell us something we don't know," Giselle says, light-heartedly.

We are all light-hearted and light-headed.

No more school for at least six weeks.

"**YOWZA**!" shouts Rob, and he sits back down next to Giselle who is combing her long brown hair.

(Just so you know my brother, Pete, assures me that the word YOWZA in a game of scrabble gives a score of twenty and it is an officially accepted word for amazement.)

Rob is now so close to Giselle that he can hear the static caused by the brushing, crackle in her hair. Giselle does have very beautiful hair and today, the first day of the summer break, Rob and Pete seem to be especially mesmerised by its beauty in the sunshine this morning. Giselle is one of those lucky girls who now only has to brush her hair to have our boys' full attention. She really is not interested in their predicament and certainly has not started brushing her hair for their pleasure but merely because it needs it.

To remind you all of what we look like, here is Giselle on your left and Claire on your right, with me, Lucy, in the middle.

From our exciting time in Sloping Meadow, when Monaie's dad saved all of our lives by skilfully crash-landing the light aircraft, (a small Lear Jet), to this very day we have all remained in contact with Monaie and her dad and with each other.

Perhaps, more importantly, we have been in constant contact with Sloping Meadow: that sweeping and majestic place we all love to visit where Monaie and her dad live with Benjamin, their donkey.

We have all managed to get through the Spring Term at school and are all very much still friends.

Monaie's dad appears with Monaie and leaves her with us.

"Take good care of my girl," he says.

"She's our girl as well," Claire responds, and she means it. Monaie has become very important to us.

Monaie smiles and there is no doubt that she is also beautiful with her long, dark, wavy hair falling just below her waist. She has dark brown glassy eyes and looks intelligent.

"Lucy," Monaie asks me, with her very special eyes, "can I please sit next to you?"

"Of course, you may," I respond, making room for her and stroking her hair as she passes me. I will let you into a secret and tell you that now that I have become firm friends with Monaie, I enjoy pulling her hair gently when she is in front of me and not expecting it. She always turns around and smiles. She is wearing thin black trousers that look like tight jeans and a top that is bright red with a long rose on the side. On her feet she has patented black leather boots that sparkle with their newness. Monaie has confided in me that she wishes to have a career in Fashion Design. I am impressed that she knows what she wants to do at six years of age.

The sun is out and is gently persuading us to feel its warmth. When it is out, it is so welcoming. I think that the sun when it is shining energises us, almost like it does to lizards in the summer. What do you think?

Rob has brought some long rope with him because today we are near the end of Stratton Common and intend on tying it to a branch of a tree and making it into a rope swing. We all climb through a gap in the fence at the end of Stratton Common as the trees near the river are higher and stronger there to make our rope swing a success.

"Shall I climb this one?" Rob asks Pete; Giselle and he both signal with a thumbs up that the chosen Elm tree looks strong enough and high enough to make a great rope swing that will hold all our weights. Before I continue, I should point out that we intend to have the rope swing not to go anywhere too near the river or it would be dangerous in view of the strong current of the River Bede as well as its depth, but to swing safely above only the ground below the Elm tree.

Monaie is excited and we promise that she may be first on it when it is constructed.

Rob begins his ascent of the tree with the long rope wrapped around his waist freeing up his hands so that he can climb, but events then take a different turn.

Pete, who has just helped Monaie through the tight gap in the fence bringing her in riverside, turns around when he hears a man desperately climbing the very same fence. He is too big to slip through the low gap that we have all managed to come through easily.

The lean man is looking anxious but otherwise seems quite friendly and normal. He climbs over the fence with great difficulty, or so it appears, especially as he looks clumsy in his efforts to raise himself up and then over. He seems 'all fingers and thumbs' as Mum says.

Pete asks, "Are you alright, sir?"

"I was alright until my Poodle came through here and will not come back to safety."

The man looks at Pete like he is about thirty-five and keen not to frighten us so he adds,

"Look, I have his leash here with me. I was meant to be taking him for a walk, a safe walk, when he ran after something. Once I get him back, I will be okay."

Rob shouts down from the tree,

"Is your Poodle large and black?"

"Why, yes," responds the man. The man is tall and thin with a beard and has shorts on. He is wearing glasses and is holding a dog's leash.

"He's in the River Bede! He is now large and black **and wet**. Very wet!"

The man immediately looks panicked and rushes too fast over to where Rob has signalled his dog is. The black Poodle is swimming in the river but looks like it is now struggling with the current. The man now slips sideways down the light brown clay and for a while it looks like he will not fall in if he can just keep his balance... but he cannot.

He slides unceremoniously onto his back, now skidding over the darker mud, straight into the deep brown waters of the River Bede and then shouts simultaneously at Pete,

"Can't swim! Can't swim! **Get help!**"

Rob reverses down the trunk of the Elm tree, then leaps from near the base of the tree and into action.

He throws the majority of the rope over to the man, holding tightly on to one end, and the rope misses him. The man is beginning to slosh and slide about in the moving waters. His dog comes near him but is also sloshing and sliding about in the waters. They both look like they are in serious trouble. Claire, our best swimmer, looks like she is mentally preparing herself to dive in and try to save the man when the second throw from Rob this time almost lands on the man's head. The man now grabs the rope tightly.

Now Pete and Rob as well as Claire, Giselle and I all hold onto the rope end and we pull and pull on it until the man is pulled to the riverbank where we then keep pulling until he can grab hold of some nearby tree branches to help himself out. Our hands have all suffered by the roughness of the strong rope and they feel stiff. Our arm muscles now also ache with the sheer effort of trying to pull a fully-grown, wet man out of the cold water. He must be twelve stone, I think.

Dripping wet and feeling very cold, he clambers out but not before pushing the back of his wet dog up the side of the muddy riverbank, until it is also saved. Both the man and dog are splattered now with dark mud. As the man wipes his brow, he smears his face with dark brown mud and we struggle not to laugh at his face or his drenched clothing. He looks weird now as some of the dark mud has sabotaged the clean cut of his beard, which now looks dishevelled and mostly half-shaved. One of his legs now looks like he has dressed in one solitary woman's stocking because of the way the dark brown mud has covered most of his leg up to his top mid-thigh.

"Lucy," directs my older brother Pete, "try not to laugh, even if you think he looks hilarious. The poor man has just nearly drowned in the River Bede! **LU-CY!**"

I am now having great difficulty in stifling a loud laugh that is doing its level best to surface from deep down in my belly, especially as I now spot his solitary mud stocking that he seems to be wearing very awkwardly.

The dog now shivers, then shakes itself and further splatters the man with dirty water and mud, much to our perverse pleasure.

"Thank you, boys, oh, and girls," he shouts above the sounds of our now muffled laughter and the gushing waters, trying desperately to flick some of the mud out of his eyes.

"I will phone for an ambulance," Pete says smiling and he does.

The man is now shivering. He looks very sad now and pale.

Mum says it is very easy for a person to catch pneumonia after falling into a river, and I guess that is why Pete was so keen to phone for an ambulance. As you may know, pneumonia is a lung infection that can make you feel very sick and often requires hospitalisation.

After what seems like a long time, the ambulance arrives. The two female ambulance drivers thank all of us for helping the man and his Poodle but they also tell us off for being on the wrong side of the fence that is there to keep persons safely away from the fast-moving River Bede. For myself, I just find that this is typical of grown-ups; they are pleased on the one hand that we have saved two lives but are still keen on the other hand to find an excuse to tell us all off.

The older lady, who was driving the ambulance, informs us all, but has a knack of just looking at me when speaking:

"The River Bede is very deep with very strong currents and, over the years, many have lost their lives in it. Today you got lucky but tomorrow who knows?"

We feel rather embarrassed to have been told off by this lady especially since we have just helped save someone and their Poodle, but she becomes even more annoyed with us when she notices (a) that we are all laughing now and (b) that we have taken little Monaie with us through the gap in the fence.

"And this little one has no business," she continues, pointing at Monaie, "none whatsoever… to have been on this side of the fence! **What were you thinking?**"

Giselle tries to help by saying, "We are sorry but if we just do nothing all day in the summer holidays, we will become bored so we thought we would make a rope swing. We did not mean to cause any trouble for you. We were merely trying to find constructive things to do with our time."

The lady responds by saying,

"Look, you have done a great thing today and saved a man's life. Let's leave it at that. It must have been meant that you were here today so we will say no more."

Monaie chips in with: "We also saved the man's dog."

The lady chooses wisely not to respond to this remark but merely glares harshly at Monaie and then at us instead, when she remembers that Monaie is younger than us. I imagine that this lady rarely smiles, or so it seems to me on that summer's day on the very first day of our summer break.

The ambulance driver is keen to ensure that the man receives the best care available so, after the usual time spent inside the ambulance checking his heart and calming him, the ambulance then speeds off with sirens ablaze and is gone in moments.

Mum has told me before that the River Bede runs eventually to the River Thames and that eventually runs out into the sea and because it is all running into the sea, it can be treacherous as it picks up speed before merging with the sea. Certainly, we are glad that the man's life and that of his dog have been saved. Mum tells me that the currents in the river are hazardous especially to those who cannot swim. The man must be feeling lucky that we were all there to assist him in his time of need.

We are to meet that man again in different circumstances later on. I shall explain everything.

My memory of how things are to develop is good or at least I think so and that is all that matters to me as it is, after all, my story.

I shall tell my story in the best way that I can so that it not only pleases you but also me when I look back on it and think how well I have remembered it.

Does that sound cool to you?

Chapter 2
An Unexpected Meeting

We are still happy that we have been able to help the man yesterday on the River Bede.

This afternoon, however, we are keen to make our way over to Monaie's home so we can once again visit Sloping Meadow in its full summer glory.

Monaie's dad is in full agreement that we can all come and go as we please to Sloping Meadow for the rest of this summer. He was particularly pleased that, earlier in the spring, we had been instrumental in putting the nasty Stratton brothers away in prison for all their bad deeds. They each received four years' imprisonment for obtaining money by deception and for various crimes that included theft and burglary of other people's property.

On occasions, I still find Monaie's dad a bit intimidating but generally I am very impressed with him for saving our lives in April by being just the best possible pilot that he could have been.

Walking around Monaie's yard at the back, leading down to Sloping Meadow, we are now welcomed by the most wonderful mauve flowers. Poppies are in full bloom and they are also wonderful. Pete, my brother, photographs some of them so you can share their beauty.

A few days ago, Monaie's dad told me, "Every one of these lovely mauve Poppies came from seeds years and years ago, planted by my great aunt, Sheila Butterworth; a great lady who also dried Lavender in underground vats, in my house in the basement, where the casement window used to be left wide open all year round to help the bundles of cut Lavender thoroughly dry."

How cool are these wonderful Poppies?

Moving around the back end of the garden, near a brick wall, we are now confronted by what appear to be the loveliest Michaelmas Daisies. Mum would have loved seeing these.

Again, Pete has taken this photo with his phone so you can see why we love Sloping Meadow so much. This is really where I personally believe Sloping Meadow begins; up near Monaie's Brick Wall, as we now call it. Follow that old brick wall all the way down and you will eventually find Monaie's Gate as we now know it.

Unless you can actually make it there yourself, and you know I really hope that one day you may do so, you will not know just how great the scent of all the flowers is, especially when the sun feels hot and some slight breeze whaffs that rich scent around. It is what my mum calls being in heaven.

It is as if each flower holds heaven within itself.

Giselle has brought her sketching pad, so that she can draw some of the flowers, which she does. She is the best at drawing in her class and often, when I am permitted to see inside her class on those occasions that I go and meet her at her school, I spot her drawings on display on the classroom walls. Each one is in her distinctive, dainty style. How cool is that? She even remembers to sign her drawings which Mum tells me is good practice for an artist, otherwise others may say that they drew the artworks and claim them for themselves. So all you budding artists out there listen to my mum and sign all your works of art clearly and neatly once you have drawn your artworks.

Rob and Pete are playing catch with a yellow tennis ball when Giselle asks us all if we can change location so she can try to draw some of the wild flowers that can be found nearer the river. To reach the river will take us about forty-five minutes; that is how long Sloping Meadow takes to walk from the start of Monaie's brick wall to the wooded area, just before the River Bede flows wide and deep.

We set off and on the way Rob shouts with joy, "Lucy, a rabbit!"

It makes me laugh because he now always calls my name when an animal or bird is spotted by him.

He does this because he knows that I love all animals and nature.

We all see it but it is too long and too big for a rabbit so I quickly conclude that it is a hare. These hares can jump up and down and box each other when the spring arrives in Sloping Meadow but this hare is merely running fast and leaping up and down the yellow and green grasses of Sloping Meadow in pure joy. In March, they act totally mad and that is where the expression 'Mad as a March Hare' comes from. The males are worse and they fight each other like standing boxers inside invisible boxing rings to try and win the hearts of the females.

It seems to me that, generally, there is a profound difference between male and female; this is especially true in Mother Nature. I mean in human beings the females generally are the ones to dress up in bright colours and strive to look good and better presented, generally speaking, whereas in Mother Nature it is almost always the males that are more brightly dressed. Take the birds, for example: the males are the ones who look spectacular not the females. Look out for a male Blackbird and they are radiant whereas, by contrast, the females are brown and slightly drab. Look at the Peacock: it is the male that is resplendent with his colourful feathers.

We continue on down, past clumps of bracken and thistles in the ground; they are tall and thin like bearded priests waiting patiently for a church service to begin. Here and there are Cowslips and Bluebells: the Cowslips are early and the Bluebells are late, for around here anyway.

Monaie's dad told me once that once upon a time in the history of Sloping Meadow, no Bluebells grew here but then one year, as if by magic, following a sudden storm in the February sky, they appeared early one May and have always appeared ever since. He told me,

"They were carried by the winds in the very core of the storm and deposited straight onto the soils of Sloping Meadow where they took root and now grow here every year with majesty."

We are just happy to be here now in the vast rolling hillside that is Sloping Meadow and happy to feel the sun on our faces. Pete says the sun is almost ninety-three million miles away from our planet and yet we can feel its heat from here. How cool is that? Or rather how hot is that? Our sun is a star in every sense of the word. Well, that's what my brother Pete says all the time to me.

We rest for a few moments to take water, then, after a short walk through shorter, tougher grass, we reach the end of Sloping Meadow and the beginning of the river area. The bottoms of our jeans are dappled with the wetness from the long grasses. It soon becomes apparent that only the fronts of our jeans are wet and not the backs. Walk through long wet grass and your jeans will only become wet on the side you walk on. Trust me.

Evidence now comes that we are near the River Bede because the grasses have become taller and the soil beneath our feet softer and wetter. The river's noise can be deafening, especially at this time of year. Like Rob's whistling we can hear it before we see the source. Mosquitoes, or as Pete calls them 'midges', appear now as they always have done since the creation of the river and the birth of what we know as our

Sloping Meadow. Between the very bottom of long grasses, I spot what to me looks like a ginger shrew scuttling down into the earth between the grass roots. It is way too fast for me to follow it for long.

If we lift up any flat logs, we can now find Slow Worms: these are called legless lizards locally but are long thin snakes that always look to me like they are metallic. Their bodies can be silver or even copper coloured. Whenever you are near rivers or wetlands or even in allotments away from water, if you lift up the flat bark or flat logs (or even discarded pieces of roofing felt), you may spot some tiny baby toads or even some Slow Worms and sometimes I have seen three or four baby toads all very near three or four Slow Worms. Please do not disturb them too much and then very carefully put the piece of bark or log back where you found it. When the sun shines on the Slow Worms, they can move very fast as they are energised by the sun. Even Pete, my brother, has trouble catching them when they are warmed up by the sun. A word of caution however: do not even think about lifting up logs in August as Adders (or Vipers as they are also called) can bite you and are poisonous. You would have to go straight to your local hospital and tell them that you have been bitten by an Adder or Viper. This snake has a 'V' on its neck to help you identify it. We have Grass Snakes in Sloping Meadow, and often Pete and I have seen them swimming very fast on the surface of the water in a never-ending 'S' shape as their bodies move swiftly across the water. Monaie's dad has told us that, apart from the Slow Worms, which remember are more like legless lizards, there are, in the United Kingdom, only three types of snake: the Viper or Adder, which is poisonous, the Grass Snake which is mostly harmless and the Smooth Snake which is very rare.

Without wishing to put anyone off the Grass Snake, it can release a very bad smelling liquid from its glands on its body if caught by one of its enemies but then so too can a fully grown Toad as once I picked up a large Toad and he released a load of bad smelling water from glands near his ears and it quickly encouraged me to carefully place him immediately back from where I had picked him up. A Grass Snake, for example, if trying to capture and eat a large Toad would be quickly encouraged to let it go as this fluid excreted by the Toad is foul-tasting, or so my nature books tell me.

The River Bede flows majestically with all the splendour and the grandeur of a king: all the while becoming faster and faster and grander and grander as it nears the Thames, then merges with the Thames and then after a great number of miles flows fast southwards into the open sea to submerge itself within the sea. When the merge of the two rivers occurs, no one can tell which is the River Bede and which the River Thames. They become one fast flowing river; inseparably linked the one to the other. We are doing our best now to come to terms with the sheer volume of water powered by the mighty River Bede. This river has no intention of slowing down, as we do, when the sun gets hotter. It will keep flowing no matter what; incessantly. White surf appears on the surface caused by the sheer forces of the combined rivers. The surface bubbles continuously form then pop into tiny particles of foam; white, clear foam.

I spot a Kingfisher flash by in a haze of brilliant blue and although I urge the others to capture its image in their eye lens, none of them does. This is not all I spot, however.

"Look," I exclaim, "**The man from yesterday!** This time he is in the river again, happily **swimming!**"

Rob says, "**WOW!** He is measuring something. Lucy, he has a sort of control box in his hand and is holding it up and pointing it down at the swirling waters."

Pete is always the curious, intelligent one and can no longer control his curiosity, and shouts over,

"**Hey**, thought you said you couldn't swim, sir."

The thin long man is shocked to see us and blushes. He may have thought that he was alone today. After some time deliberating with himself, he eventually decides to acknowledge, then respond to us.

"Oh dear! It's a long and dark story. May I dry first then meet you up where you are?"

"Yes, I suppose you may, if you intend on doing just that," replies Pete, annoyed with him for pretending that he could not swim and causing an unnecessary rescue yesterday. Pete screws his eyes up in sheer disgust at this man who wasted not only our time by lying but also the ambulance crew's time.

The man swims skilfully to the riverbank, places his control box into a dry leather case and walks over now, carrying the case and at the same time, frantically trying to dry himself. We are intrigued as to what he will have to say for himself now. He can see the annoyance written on our sun-kissed faces. To me, he seems to approach us all now with a certain uncharacteristic caution.

Giselle, in particular, is very annoyed with him and says,

"Do you **always** ask people to help rescue you from drowning when in fact there is no need to, because you can swim very well, actually?"

"I… I try not to. Look, I am sorry about that but when you hear me out, you will agree that I had no choice but to…"

"**Lie**? Is that how you wished to end your sentence? With the word lie? I am not sure we will be in the right mood to agree on anything with you for some time to come," she adds emphatically, turning her head away from him dramatically. She then sweeps her long hair to completely cover her face and stands with her back to him in defiance and her legs apart in what I can only describe as a powerful pose. She is so interesting when she is angry. Her nostrils have opened up with the sheer annoyance of his presence. She then takes in a very deep breath as though to increase her inner strength. I do not blame her for being upset with this man especially when I remember my sore hands and arms from pulling the rope yesterday, with him on the other end pretending not to be able to swim. When, finally, she slowly releases her breath out of her mouth, she looks now a formidable adversary for him and he certainly acknowledges this fact with a forced smile.

Nonetheless, the man's body language quickly demonstrates to us all, however, that he is apologetic and full of regret at having to lie to us. He is probably guilty that he has caused us to act out a ridiculous rescue on him when he did not appear to need it. I, for one, shall be interested in just what he will say to us that could possibly make us think differently about him or his character.

Giselle is supremely angry; she, like us, has every right to be so. Her green eyes scan him carefully.

How annoying this man has become in the space of a few hours.

He is not cool.

Chapter 3
North Is So Much Different to the South

We now sit quietly by the riverbank. We are now eager to hear just what this man will come up with next.

"My name is Bora and I was born in South Kortana. I went to study in London and even managed to obtain a first class honours degree in Education at Kingston University. Later, I went to work in North Kortana but the situation there is impossible now. There is very little in the way of food for ordinary people and the government there will destroy anyone who speaks out against the leader.

"My dear friend, Professor Sebastian Mendoza, born in Peru, is a brilliant scientist who specialises in Nuclear Power. With his vast knowledge, he is now making Nuclear Bombs and Nuclear Warheads for North Kortana to use against their so-called enemies. He is now very keen to defect to England where he will help England understand just how different North Kortana is from South Kortana. Basically, he wants out."

"What does defect mean?" I ask him. I am never shy about asking the meaning of words I am not sure of and neither should any of you be. We all have to learn new things and what better way than of using your voice box and asking.

He asks me my name. I tell him.

"Lucy, from what little I know, to 'defect' means to give up your country for someone else's because you are totally fed up with the bad people running the country."

"And who are these bad people?" I ask.

"They are the ones currently running the country," Bora continues, "They have made it very hard for the ordinary people who do not have enough food and are starving. Many of the population have at times resorted to eating grass as they are out of proper food. What the leaders want to do is have Nuclear Bombs, which cost huge sums of money, so they can impress, then threaten other countries with them and threaten wars with their neighbours, South Kortana and other countries, like Japan, and even the USA. Professor Mendoza is desperate to leave North Kortana, but they will kill him if he is caught trying to escape."

"So, what has this to do with you swimming today in the River Bede?" Giselle asks impatiently, turning only part of her face towards him. He sees only her profile with glaring green eyes now as she has deliberately tilted her head towards him in a clear message of contempt.

Giselle's eyes now glare directly at Bora. Bora cannot face looking at her and his eyes now hold embarrassment within them. He looks away as though intimidated by her justified anger.

"I am working for Professor Mendoza who is desperate to leave North Kortana; so desperate in fact that he will risk his only daughter coming to this country first to check out the route."

"The route?" Pete asks.

"Well, I was checking the depth of the water for a reason."

"What reason could you possibly need to check the depth of the water, unless the Professor's daughter is swimming here from North Kortana?" Claire asks, sarcastically. We laugh at her sarcasm but it is more in a nervous response to the situation.

It is uncharacteristic of Claire to be sarcastic. Mum always says that "sarcasm is the lowest form of wit".

"Not swimming exactly," replies Bora, sheepishly.

"Look," Giselle then says angrily, "my friends and I risked our necks saving your life and that of your wretched, drowning dog, so you can't hold back anymore! I almost jumped into the water with my clothes on for you, to save you! We are not prepared to listen to any more lies and will walk away from you. Now, do you choose to speak the truth or some more of your lies?"

"Beatriz Mendoza is also risking her life coming here first to ensure it is a safe journey for her father to make."

"Most planes are safe," replies Rob, as dry as a desert.

"You do not understand. There is no way that the Professor is able to go to an airport like most people in your country. He is a very well-known face in North Kortana. He is working on Nuclear Science and will not be permitted to travel. He has his passport held by the North Kortanese Military. They will never allow him to leave North Kortana. The only way is by a completely different and unexpected means."

"**By swimming**?" Giselle says, rolling her eyes upwards into her brows, still looking wonderfully annoyed with Bora and not for the first time. We smile at her humour now.

I have noticed that her nostrils are still open and this gives her an angry face. In her anger she is, to me, still very attractive. I think to myself, *Wow! Giselle is awesome today!*

"Swimming is involved at some point," Bora says sheepishly.

"At some point? At **which** point?" Giselle now demands to know.

"At the end point," Bora says with a very serious face.

"Which is?" I now demand to know.

"Which is here, Lucy," he replies.

"**Here**?" we all shout, incredulously, as it dawns on us that he really does mean here.

"Why here? Why the River Bede?" We are with one voice.

"The submarine can, according to…" Bora says.

"**The what**?" we all chip in.

"If I may continue, please. The submarine, because of the depths of the water in the River Bede, can come from the North Atlantic Ocean and travel eastwards into the River Thames until it comes to meet the River Bede. You are the best chance Beatriz Mendoza will have of making it safely in what is still a very long and dangerous journey. We know the submarine can easily travel fast up the Thames but we are not risking her clamouring out of it in the heart of London. Too many faces to see her and possibly photograph and report her to the North Kortanese and then…"

Pete says, "And then what?"

"Big trouble if they send out their spies here."

"Oh great," Pete says, "so we needlessly save your life and now will have to face great trouble again. Just why should we do this and help you for people we do not even know?"

"You will also be doing it for your country's good. Your government will learn much about North Kortana and its impossibly harsh regime. You will learn so much about what stage they are up to in being able to put nuclear weapons onto small and large rockets. Need I go on?"

"We are children; we need more than you have given us." Giselle has spoken and Bora instinctively knows that he must give us more than he has already, or risk more anger from Giselle. Giselle has been very assertive today and will not be beaten by this man. This man really only has one last chance.

"Well, let me describe Beatriz Mendoza."

"Haven't you a photo of her, or is she made up as well?" Giselle asks.

"Why, as a matter of fact, I do. I do have a photograph of her with me. Please allow me to locate it."

Bora shows us a photo of her that he is carrying in his wallet. Pete quickly takes a photo of it so you can now see what she looks like.

Giselle swiftly changes from anger to softness when she takes in the photograph. Her anger only now begins to subside as her true and caring side shines out. She is generally slow to anger and is enjoying returning to her usual self, still enigmatic but no longer angry.

"Eh... how old is... the... girl with a parrot?" she slowly asks.

"The Princess is about ten I believe," he replies.

"**The Princess**?" Giselle shouts.

She is definitely shocked, as we all are. In one moment she has changed from being the girl with a parrot to being a princess.

"Oh dear, I may have said too much. In her father's country, Peru, she is entitled to be called a princess as she descends from the Royal Peruvian Family."

"Does she still have the parrot?" I ask, predictably.

"Yes, and I believe when she travels here, she will insist on bringing it in the submarine."

Bora then says to us that he regrets that he has not been honest with us before but, if he had been, he may have blown his cover at a time when he was not sure that he could trust us.

"And do you, now?" I ask.

"And do I what, Lucy? Trust you now? Yes," he replies.

"Just how do you think you will manage to move a submarine all around the coasts of China, Hong Kong, Vietnam, Thailand, India, through the Suez Canal in Egypt, past Turkey, Greece, Italy and Spain, not to mention France and Belgium, or indeed England, without any of those countries noticing it or picking it up on their radar?" Pete says, after consulting Google on his iPhone, to make quite sure of the places he was referring to.

"Who said the Princess Beatriz Mendoza was going to travel that way?" Bora declared.

"There is no other way, is there?" Pete asks.

"Oh, yes there is. The Professor has decided to go the other way. The submarine will travel deep from North Kortana through the Sea of Japan, past Japan, through the Sea of Okhotsk around to the Bering Sea, East Siberian Sea, then to the Laptey Sea, Kara Sea, Barents Sea, to the Norwegian Sea, past Norway, then through the middle of the Shetlands, past Ireland and around Southampton to London-the River Thames-up the River Thames and along the River Bede to here."

Pete then cries out, "Princess Beatriz is basically then coming all the way around massive Russia, where there are very few controls to check for submarines and into our River Bede. Here?"

"Correct. Remember that Professor Mendoza is a Professor of Nuclear Power so he has designed these submarines which are currently being tested thoroughly by the North Kortanese Military. They are Nuclear Submarines, capable of great speed. They also have the ability to almost make themselves invisible to radar once powered up and running but the path around Russia will be far less dangerous and far less people to detect their passage by satellite. No one will expect a submarine, a nuclear submarine, to travel in the direction that Princess Beatriz will take."

"But he can't just get the North Kortanese Military to agree to one of these being used to ferry his daughter, Princess Beatriz, here," Rob asks, "can he?"

"Oh, yes he can; he has friends who will help him."

"How do you know they will not let him down?"

"They cannot let him down now," Bora says.

"But how are you so sure?" Rob asks.

"Because I have heard from the submarine today, two hours ago in fact, when it was just outside the coast of Ireland. I have confirmed already that the depth of the River Bede is suitable to safely carry the submarine. They are on their way. Now the question is: are you able to help Princess Beatriz when she arrives? She will need somewhere safe to stay and must be kept completely hidden until her father arrives much later in the week; if she confirms to him that all is well. He is ill and she has therefore volunteered to make the journey so that she may tell him if she thinks he can make it or not. The Princess will stay in this country; whatever she decides for her father. The Professor wants her out of North Kortana. This is why the Princess has chosen to take her pet parrot with her. It is because she will remain in the UK. If then it is okay for the Professor to make the journey, then they can both go to the British Home Office together and can claim asylum."

My dear brother Pete explains to me that 'asylum' is where people arriving in any country are able to claim a place of safety there until everything is considered very carefully and the persons are either accepted into the country or not. In the event they are refused entry into a country, they will be returned to their own. This option does not bear thinking about for the Mendozas.

"Do we have a choice?" Rob asks.

"Yes, you do. You always have a choice in life. You can agree to help the Princess or agree not to help her. In the event you decide to help, there will certainly be a risk of harm or danger."

Bora then looks at all of us one by one with pleading eyes, and slowly our hearts begin to melt, like butter on toast.

Claire looks around at our faces and says, "If it was one of us, what would we want?"

"To be helped," I say.

"Then, Lucy, that is exactly what we need to do," Pete and Rob say. "We will agree to help."

Monaie says, "Yes. Lucy, you are correct."

We all smile at her, and Bora also now smiles at everyone: masking his fear for the future very well. He immediately begins to unpack torches and what look like diving suits and then some sort of radio transmitter. He hides these under a clump of bushes. We agree to meet him here, exactly here, at night, at eight p.m. We decide quickly that we will involve Monaie's dad but to the other parents we will have to say that we are all having a sleepover at Monaie's.

Monaie smiles for the second time in a minute. She will be very pleased to help us so that we may be in a position to help Princess Beatriz.

I rush through my supper and tell Mum I am staying for a sleepover at Monaie's. Mum instructs me to have a good time and I thank her. At the same time, I think,

A real princess. How cool is that?

And, you know, I am delighted to be in a position to help this Princess.

All of us agree to meet at seven-thirty p.m. at Monaie's house so we can discuss the whole exciting business with Monaie's dad, mostly to seek his advice and guidance, before we meet Bora at eight p.m.

I am well excited.

Chapter 4
Cometh the Hour

We knock at the door and when we do Monaie's dad immediately says,

"Come in, all of you. I am just listening to piano concerto number two in C minor by Rachmaninov; a very famous composer of classical music. I hope you can appreciate the beautiful sounds in his music."

We are far too excited to actually stop and listen to what sounds quite good to our ears. When you can, try to listen to this piece of music and I think you will not only see why Monaie's dad likes it but you may learn to like it for yourself.

He continues, "And just how can I help you, because Monaie has already told me that you may need my assistance on something special?"

He winks at me, still slightly unsettling me when I think back to his past when he saw the 'Mermaid at Sea' when he was twenty.

Pete says, unable to control his beaming smile, "Please sit down first and please... relax."

Monaie's dad both sits and relaxes as the beautiful music plays on his CD player. He lights his sweet-smelling tobacco in his favourite pipe. The air is filled with a sweet aromatic flavour as the subject is raised gently against a fitting background of classical music.

It is I who begins to set out our stall as they say.

"Yesterday, we saved a man's life in the river and he told us all that he could not swim so we all struggled to save him and hurt our hands doing it and today we met him again; only today he is a great swimmer, as we found out. There was a very good reason for him not to blow his cover. He is an official from North Kortana and is desperate. Desperate to help his friend, Professor Mendoza, a great Scientist, who although currently helping North Kortana build Nuclear Bombs and rockets to carry them, wants to, what was the word, Pete?"

Pete informs loudly, "**Defect.**"

I continue, "He wants to defect to our country but because he is ill, he needs to send his daughter, a real princess, to us first to check out the route and see if it is possible for him to journey here safely."

"To see if what is possible?" Monaie's dad asks.

"To see," Pete says, "if the Nuclear Submarine can make it around the continent of Russia and all the other coastlines on the way to arrive safely here."

"To arrive safely **where**?" Monaie's dad now insists to know.

"To arrive safely in the River Bede just behind Stratton Common if you must know," Pete responds.

"And I thought Monaie said that it was something special!" Monaie's dad jokes, making smoke rings with his mouth. Even now Monaie's dad is thinking deeply about what he has just heard and, largely due to his experience of sailing around the world, he knows that there will be danger in what he has just heard. It is not a task for the faint-hearted.

For now Monaie's dad keeps his fears to himself.

We all laugh, except Monaie, who smiles sweetly at her dad.

Claire informs, "The Princess Beatriz will need somewhere to stay until her father arrives here later in the same submarine once it has returned to North Kortana and collected him."

Monaie's dad winks at Claire in his best pirate way.

"And… let me guess, you would like Monaie and I to put this Princess up here and look after her at Sloping Meadow?" he asks.

"Not just her," Monaie says.

"Not just her?" Monaie's dad now tickles Monaie playfully making her giggle.

"No, Dad, she has a parrot." Monaie declares with joy in her heart.

"Oh, I should have guessed if it was anything to do with you guys," Monaie's dad says, and then we laugh loud and long. This time Monaie joins in.

The relief we all feel that Monaie's dad can and will help us look after Princess Beatriz is tremendous.

Monaie's dad then states, "Well, Monaie, looks like we need to get a room ready for the Princess and her parrot, and make up a bed and possibly a perch for the parrot. You can help me, honey."

"Of course I will, Dad," she replies beaming with joy, uncertain if her dad was joking about the perch for the parrot.

We are now all beaming with joy at the prospect of meeting the Princess, but my joy is greater as I am also looking forward to meeting the parrot as well. And you can only guess just how much I am looking forward to meeting a real princess.

We say our farewells and Pete takes Monaie's dad's mobile phone number and places it on his phone, just in case we ever need it.

What a happy time we have spent at Monaie's home.

In all fairness, I must point out that none of us is aware of the danger that we face now in agreeing to help the girl with a parrot, Princess Beatriz.

Chapter 5
Depths of Joy

We now race back to the very end of Sloping Meadow, passing those beautiful mauve Poppies again and this time rush past the wonderful Roses, deep red Roses, smelling divine, near the end of their short green lawns. For a fleeting moment, we all are entranced by the perfume emanating from these roses. We end up running fast towards our meeting point and just as it turns to eight p.m., we all arrive, panting and excited.

I explain to Bora the good news that Monaie's dad has agreed that the Princess will be looked after at Sloping Meadow. He is overjoyed. He gives me a hearty hug.

Bora then tells us, "There is a hitch. The submarine has encountered difficulties negotiating one of the mouths of underground caves before entering the River Thames but now is making its way up the River Bede. The ETA, sorry the Estimated Time of Arrival, is now eight fifteen p.m. tonight due to very slight damage."

"Only fifteen minutes late for a journey of such distance is remarkable, is it not?" Rob says, and we all agree with him.

"Professor Mendoza is a perfectionist and would have preferred a rendezvous of eight p.m. precisely."

"Does rendezvous mean meeting point?"

"Yes, Lucy," Bora replies smiling, "It comes from the French. Well done, Lucy."

I smile and Pete looks at his watch impatiently.

Giselle says, "Just why are boys so impatient? They will arrive soon."

"We are not impatient," cries Rob.

"Oh, yes you are. All the males I know are impatient. My dad, my grandad, you and Pete… and even, I guess, Monaie's dad."

"We are so not," argues Rob.

"You are so!" Giselle responds.

"We are not," Pete says, "we just like things to happen when we are expecting them to."

While this is going on, Bora asks for "hush now" as we begin to hear a throbbing sound in the water.

It is only in a whisper that the smiling Bora is willing to concede, "There is some truth in what Giselle has just said about males."

Looking down we can hear a sort of swishing from inside the very depths of the river; a sound that is now growing louder and louder. We can see swirls of water crashing up the sides of the two riverbanks, drenching the dry mud at the top of the riverbanks. Anticipation hangs in the air. All of us feel the excitement of expectation: we expect to see a real princess and her parrot, we expect some sort of a mechanical device to rise up out of the River Bede, and we expect to feel great joy when we all meet her, the real Princess from Kortana.

Bora grabs his torch and begins putting on a wet suit that makes us laugh as the more he puts on the more he resembles a large thin frog with its legs fully extended. His flippers look like a frog's webbed feet.

"Please, children, please do not laugh at me," he implores.

However, the more he asks us not to laugh, the more we want to giggle and laugh.

Giselle is now crying with laughter and we all join in. Rob and Pete, I notice, are shaking with the effort of trying to hold it in. Finally, we just blurt out the laughter inside us all and then even Bora, who has tried to remain serious, now laughs with us. Bora now collapses with laughter and manages to splutter, "Okay. Children. **Enough**. Please! We have to be serious now in order to help Princess Beatriz come safely off the submarine. Giselle, please, you seem to be the worst offender."

Giselle actually finds it sweet that he has twice spoken her name so soon after he has had to put up with her anger. She privately imagines a certain softness in the way he said her name and plays it back in her mind with satisfaction. She is pleasantly confused now and smiles to herself a knowing smile. I notice this and I think, in time, she will learn to like Bora. I think I mean admire.

We all straighten our faces and pull frowns now in order to help us stop laughing. It helps and we are back as a team of helpers again.

Slowly, we can hear Bora on the radio communicating to those inside the submarine and we are amazed as the top side of the submarine begins to surface now above the water like a miracle of science.

"**WOW!**" we all say in wonder.

The top has what appears to be a flat platform and in the middle, is what appears to be like a post box, a black post box. From out of the side of this post box a heavy door clunks partly open to a grating, metallic sound and we witness a man in heavy weatherproof clothing stand outside and grip a railing to keep himself steady. On the top side of the submarine are many gadgets and aerials protruding upwards. The submarine itself is of a black metallic colour and the whole image conjures up one of sophistication and strength. This is not a pretty site. The submarine looks ugly and functional, and, dare I suggest, very masculine in design and finish. There is also a smell of engines and oil. Light appears: artificial yellow light from deep within the confines of the body of the submarine.

The door opens wider now as we watch as Bora, the frogman, simultaneously dives almost silently straight into the water from our side of the riverbank with a quiet slurping sound. He will be there to assist the Princess and her parrot in disembarking from the long submarine. The Princess appears at the same time as we spot Bora, the frogman, surfacing next to the submarine.

With great skill now we watch him lift the Princess almost off the submarine and into the air just above the water, just as easily as a ballroom dancer would lift his partner. He has to be strong to hold her horizontally above his frog suit. All of us still have problems to control our giggling as more than ever Bora now resembles a long thin frog, especially now that our long thin frog is in his natural element, water.

He gently swims over, places her on the riverbank near us and we run to help her feel safe and make her feel welcome to England. Later, he returns to the submarine to collect a long suitcase, which he again holds high above him, before passing one end of it to Pete. Pete manages to bring the suitcase onto the riverbank near us without it becoming wet.

With great swirling in the deep and dark water we watch now as the Nuclear Submarine clanks shut the door, extinguishing the artificial light now and submerges slowly into the River Bede like a long metallic fish. In moments, there is nothing to see but swirls of deep, black water. It leaves as silently as it arrived minutes earlier. A gentle mechanical throbbing now subsides to almost nothing. Only white foam remains on the surface. And even that now disappears as the bubbles of foam collapse into plain black water again. The surface of the water is now relatively calm. The noise has left us completely.

I am still dazzled at the sheer size of the submarine that we have witnessed earlier on the surface of the River Bede. It is now that we all crowd around Princess Beatriz to see just what she looks like. Once she has taken off what seem to us to be waterproof clothing, she reveals herself and the parrot she is carrying underneath her waterproofs. She is keen to allow the parrot out of the cage immediately and we then see her and the parrot in the light of Bora's torch. For all its long journey, the parrot looks calm perched on her right shoulder.

I notice now that Bora is smiling with what seems like relief; so he must have been very worried that things may not have turned out so well. With good grace now he smiles sweetly at Giselle and a certain bond of friendship and understanding has been formed at that precise moment between them, replacing the anger and the awkwardness that had, until that moment, existed as their sole relationship.

We are overjoyed that the Princess has made it safely from North Kortana, but she must be tired and hungry. Bora explains that she will be very tired but not hungry as there is a chef on board the submarine who would have fed the crew of four and her with special Kortanese delicacies, which her father would have been able to freely obtain as working for the leader.

"Am I in England... please?" she enquires sweetly, and Giselle and I squeal in delight, "Yes, Princess Mendoza."

Bora explains that whilst her English is good like his, she is, nonetheless, very tired and her tiredness will impact on her communication skills. She will need to be taken to Monaie's home to sleep and generally to acclimatise to her new surroundings, away from the endless sounds and movement in the water caused by the submarine's constantly throbbing engine.

Giselle says gently and perhaps a bit too slowly, "You are most welcome to England. You will stay with Monaie and her dad, and they are our friends. They will look after you."

The Princess nods sleepily and her eyes now darken as her pupils enlarge, instinctively preparing for sleep.

The unexpected moon appears now from the clouds as we disappear from the riverbank, closely followed by Bora and the boys.

As quickly and as quietly as we can, we walk towards our friend, Sloping Meadow, in the moonlight; tired but happy. Little do our parents realise that we are not having a sleepover at Monaie's but are receiving a guest from thousands of miles away who just happens to be a real princess. And that very special guest has come with a parrot on her shoulder.

How cool is that?

Bora thanks Monaie's dad after meeting him for all his help in allowing the Princess to stay at Sloping Meadow and then leaves for his hotel in Croydon, a nearby village.

Giselle, Claire, Monaie and I will sleep in Monaie's bedroom while the Princess and the parrot will sleep in the spare bedroom. The boys will sleep on the floor of the lounge room. We all say goodnight to each other and, to the sound of foxes screaming in the night to attract each other's attention, we fall asleep; tired but happy.

Monaie's dad falls asleep in his favourite chair in his study and all is quiet in the world. The moon stays up late like a quiet, sombre witness to the night that we took in a real princess from out of the swirling depths of the River Bede.

The River Bede is actually mentioned in the 'Doomsday Book'. This is a very old historical book that records lands and territory in England.

We all have grown to love this river over the years, especially because it has brought water to the surrounding areas, and to our lovely Sloping Meadow, which very much needs the underground and largely unseen irrigation provided by this very regal river.

All the wooden shutters of Monaie's lovely home are tightly shut and now even the moon is shuttered with large dark clouds in front of it, so that Sloping Meadow now sleeps soundly as do we all, including any princesses we are looking out for.

A solitary Barn Owl flies across the night sky barely showing its white wings under a fast disappearing moon and, without making a sound, it first skims a Cedar tree and then pounces on a small rodent in Sloping Meadow that reluctantly and unexpectedly gives up its life to feed it. The poor mouse never stood a chance with such a silent and powerful predator.

How seemingly cruel is Mother Nature at times?

We all sleep safely in the darkness of the night.

Chapter 6
Picnic at Box Hill

Morning light rudely nudges us all awake with its brightness.

Monaie's dad must have already opened the wooden shutters. The glare hurts our eyes. As we blink in this new light, our senses waken to the smell of cooking. It is not long before we all hear the loud crackle and screaming splutters of fresh farm eggs being fried in the frying pan. They sound like they are screaming for their lives.

Monaie's lovely dad is cooking for us all, and we can smell the great smell of eggs being cooked and toast, well done toast.

It's enough to even whet the appetite of a princess.

The Princess now gently wakes up wondering where on earth she is. It is not long before she hears her parrot scuttling about his cage and she then remembers the long journey and the constant sound of the submarine engine. She had found it hard to sleep every night in the submarine but now, well now, she has slept like a dormouse in the daytime sunshine. She feels very calm and only faintly recalls the long walk through Sloping Meadow and the long shadows of the tall Cedar Trees cast by the presence of the moon.

I rush into the Princess's room offering to feed her parrot and even remembering to curtsy to her in my loose nightie.

"What is your name please?" she asks me.

"I am Lucy, your majesty," I say and curtsy again, nearly tripping over the bottom of my nightie.

"Please understand that if I was in Peru, I may have expected you to curtsy, but in England I do not wish you to treat me like a princess but like a friend."

44

"Yes," I say, "I now understand that a real princess from Peru wants to be my friend!"

"No, I mean yes," she replies.

"Good, your majesty," I say, jumping for joy, then curtsying again.

"No."

"No?"

Rather nervously I quickly curtsy again, not really sure of what to do or say anymore.

"Look, I want you as my friend but not to call me a princess or treat me differently. Please can you do this as it will make me happy?"

"Yes, Princess," I reply stroking the parrot, which grabs my hair in its beak. I have a job to wrestle my hair back from the parrot. The parrot squawks noisily. The Princess giggles at my predicament.

Giselle and Claire and Monaie walk in, eager to greet her and even more eager to make friends with her. All three do their best to curtsy together. The Princess laughs loudly. All three of them have managed to curtsy very clumsily indeed.

I speak very quickly, "The Princess is happy to be friends with me."

"No. Yes. Look, what I mean is, I would like to be friends with you all but I need you to please treat me properly from now on."

"You mean," says Claire, "like a real princess. Yes, we will! We most certainly will."

This time Claire curtsies and slips forward in her onesie, making us all laugh.

"No. I want you all to treat me like a real friend and not like a real princess."

"Oh," I say, "if that is what you would like we will obey, your majesty, I mean we will all agree to do this, Princess."

To emphasise what I have just said, I then deliver a perfect curtsy.

Only then do we all realise just how funny the conversation has become and we laugh loud and long until

Monaie's dad breaks the enchanted, feminine spell by shouting up the stairs in his rich masculine voice,

"Eggs! Come and get them!"

We are ravenous and do not need telling twice. Even the Princess rushes down, forgetting all about her royal decorum and her dignity.

The boys are there already, eating theirs, when we come down stairs to the large oak kitchen table. We explain that Princess Beatriz would prefer us not treating her like a princess at all. The boys, preoccupied by their food, grunt in agreement, making all the females smile at how engrossed boys are when it comes to food. The boys feel slightly embarrassed but the moment of learning has passed them by. They only pretend to have heard what has been said to them. All the females knowingly smile together.

Monaie's dad, having eaten his own eggs and bacon now takes time to explain that: "We are all going on a picnic. To Box Hill. Roughly twelve miles away from Sloping Meadow but well worth a visit."

He will take us all in the blue horse truck and we will leave in ten minutes or just as long as it takes him to pack the sandwiches and drinks that he has prepared into the back of the blue horse truck. So, we now have a few minutes to clean our teeth and visit the loos before we go. In no time at all we are all ready to go. Rob and Pete both agree to travel in the back of the truck, in view of the limited space in the front. To them it is like an adventure. *Why is it*, I wonder, *that boys, given the choice between being more comfortable in the front on a reasonable seat would every time prefer to be thrown about in the rear with no seat in sight? To each their own*, I think.

Yes, I know, that they should be wearing seat belts but honestly if we are to worry about every little detail we would never have any adventures at all to tell our children if and when they come into our lives. Too many children are spoilt, Mum says, and all children need to have some adventures. Why, some children never have walked to school in their lives and you know what I think, they will end up unhealthy and lazy? I walk every day to my school.

How cool is that?

Chapter 7
The Upside-Down Man

The sun is up very early but it is almost eight a.m. before we finally leave Sloping Meadow for Box Hill. We are all excited.

Just before we leave, we catch sight of Benjamin the donkey in the very heart of Sloping Meadow. Pete takes a photo of him. Here he is then in the bright morning sunshine. Isn't he just so handsome? What do you think?

Princess Beatriz is thrilled that she has once again seen the donkey that Monaie owns. Monaie is also thrilled that after telling the Princess all about Benjamin the night before, she can now see him again for herself in the light of day.

Rob is whistling in the back of the truck as we leave the main road past Stratton Farm and up towards the area where Box Hill lies. It lies mostly in Dorking and is a vast area of natural beauty.

Pete has phoned my mum and asked her to let all the other parents know that we are out all day to Box Hill for a picnic with Monaie and her dad. Mum has already told me that the Scotsman who invented Television, John Logie Baird, lived for a while at the top of Box Hill and we should be able to see his former home from one of the pathways. From its summit, Box Hill has great views of the surrounding villages, so we cannot wait to show Princess Beatriz. I have been here before but not for many months.

Monaie's dad, being just like a pirate to me, is not keen to pay parking fees and so has planned where we will park. He leaves the blue horse truck right near a road called Zig-Zag Road. How cool is the name of that road? It lives up to its name, believe me, as it zig-zags for at least half a mile. In Ebbisham, a nearby village, there is a café apparently called 'ZIG ZAG' but I have never been allowed to enter it yet. Is there a link? Who knows?

We now walk along the road past Juniper Hall and turn into the entrance to a couple of farmers' fields, a small part of which is gravelled over and used as a free car park. At the back of that small car park we begin our long walk, through tall trees, then climbing slowly up, past rabbit fields on the right and soon we are then in more open countryside where the National Trust sometimes keep cattle but not small dainty cattle; huge black and white cattle with long rounded horns. They look to me menacing.

Monaie's dad says that they are harmless but later admits that the solitary bull on its own in a muddy field that we have just walked past, is anything but harmless. The bull is covered in flies but seems oblivious to them.

Two white horses, with riders on them, pass us noisily on our pathway, leaving heavy hoof marks in the drying mud. From the horses' nostrils we can see what looks like smoke but is in fact hot air from deep within their lungs hitting the cooler air of the countryside. I notice sweat on the horses' flanks.

The impression they have given is that had we not moved swiftly out of their way they would have ground us into the mud without mercy. This, of course, is an exaggeration on my part but I, for one, would not wish to have stood in their way.

We are not alone now as we can see large crows flapping up and down near the surface of the long grasses like low, black kites in the wind. I guess they are catching insects but I am too far away to see what type of insects they might be. Or, perhaps, the crows are just playing in the strong gusts of wind at the top of the fields. Who knows?

The sun, through the canopy of trees, is shining bright. We soon enter more shaded bits and then come out to what is more open lands with steep sides. The higher we reach, the more we are able to view the very tops of the Box Trees that give this place its name. Whenever we enter shade, we immediately notice the drop in temperature. Some grey squirrels scamper about the floor of the woodlands; they are young and I believe are just playing. Squirrels, as you may know, can kill each other when they fight for territory but it is usually the adults that do this. The bite from a mature squirrel can be lethal to a fellow squirrel. Any humans handling squirrels must do so with very long gloves on otherwise they will receive a very deep bite, so do be very careful if and when you choose to feed squirrels. They are wild animals, you know. Always look out for your fingers. I do.

"I love this fresh air and the country scenes, and all this greenery," Princess Beatriz informs us all.

"Yes," Claire agrees, "it is beautiful here in the base of this cool valley."

As the path meanders, it becomes rapidly steeper and muddier until we can all hear the solitary sound of Monaie's dad panting as he finds it more difficult to negotiate the climb.

Monaie keeps a tight grip on my hand and we begin to skip more with sheer joy at being here with our friends, old and new.

"My father would like it here," says Princess Beatriz.

Rob replies with, "Perhaps you can take him here when you both are settled. This is certainly one of my favourite walks. It reminds me of one of the film sets for 'The Last of the Mohicans' where the English soldiers were attacked by the Native Americans in the ravine."

"Great film, seen it three times," Pete responds, enthusiastically.

"Sounds like a boys' film," Giselle shouts.

"There is love in it," Rob says.

"Why should only females be interested in love?" Claire shouts across at him.

"And good scenery," Pete adds.

"I bet there is more action and fighting and dying in it than love and fine scenery," Claire says, unfairly, as it happens, as she has not seen the film.

"Suppose so," Rob responds, "but still a great film."

"A great boys' film," Giselle concludes.

We walk a long way, all the while climbing upwards, towards what will become the top layers of Box Hill. This really is a magnificent place with a magnificent view of miles around.

Giselle informs us all that in 'Emma', a famous book, written by Jane Austen, the characters all went for a picnic to Box Hill.

"It doesn't surprise me. It is a great place to come and walk and just breathe in the air," I say.

"Monaie, I will need to rest soon," Monaie's dad jokes.

"Dad, you can do this," Monaie tells him, and we all smile at how sweet she is towards her dad.

Two more grey and white horses with riders are spotted through a distant wooded glade and then we really are almost at the top of the Box Hill in terms of height. At the very top we carry on walking south towards an open area where we will be able to see the views over Dorking fields and Dorking Town but only if we cross a narrow, busy road.

Minutes later, we can see a lovely panoramic view of fields, sheep, railway lines and trains moving along, looking like they are toys. We are very high up here at the top of Box Hill.

"I am loving this view," Princess Beatriz exclaims, "thank you so much for this opportunity!"

Monaie's dad says, "I thought you may enjoy it here. Later, you can meet the Upside-Down Man, but first let Monaie and I and Lucy go to the National Trust Shop here and bring you ice cream tubs and we can all look at the view while we eat them."

We went to the shop where you can see inside a real working beehive and are protected from the bees by glass and where you can sit around and enjoy the area. Monaie was transfixed by the sheer number of bees inside the glass case. We then brought the ice cream tubs back to the others and we all enjoyed the ice cream then made our way to where the Scotsman, John Logie Baird, the inventor of Television, once lived. His former home is near the shop. Do try and ask your parents or guardians to take you here so you can share what we have enjoyed. We see many men, women and children on bicycles which shows just how popular Box Hill is in summer.

Then we walked on around the corner, deep behind the National Trust Shop, and on to the narrow paths that lead to the Upside-Down Man.

The Upside-Down Man was an eccentric, local man, who, when alive, left instructions that he wanted to be buried down vertically as it were rather than horizontally at the very top of Box Hill, and so his friends and the local authorities agreed to do this for him as his last wish. You can see his gravestone at the top of Box Hill. Underneath, his body is actually buried head down, if the rumours are true. It must have taken more than a few men to carry his coffin up to the top of Box Hill. I think they must have slipped often on the damp chalk paths. Or perhaps they used a horse and cart? Who knows?

We carry on down narrow, muddy pathways towards the small, open chalk pits, containing short grasses and then find ourselves in a beautiful expanse of very short green grasses where we are able now to look down and see Zig-Zag Road and the blue horse truck. It is the rabbits, I believe, that keep the grass short here. Evidence that they are about at dusk and during the night is to be seen, by their small black droppings. While we are walking above them, they are a few feet only underneath us; all snuggled up and perhaps sleeping. Without a doubt they must hear our footsteps above.

There is now a vast, sloping, short grass bank all the way to the bottom of Box Hill, where the roads are and it is here we decide, neither halfway up nor halfway down, to enjoy our picnic. From here we can see wonderful views of the vineyards across the eastern side and even the house and grounds of Juniper Hall further down. It is a very hot day now as the sun is reaching its full height, what experts term its zenith, which means its very best or highest point in the sky. What little cloud populated the sky has now drifted elsewhere and we have a lovely blue sky over Dorking. Mum says when you are in Dorking, it does not seem very green at all but when you are at the top of Box Hill, you can clearly see just how much greenery, land and trees surround this beautiful area.

We are so lucky to be here and free, not like some people and children in the world who, even now, while I am telling you this, are perhaps suffering all sorts of difficulties. This is why I believe we should always keep in mind that there are many others in this world who, when we are happy are perhaps very sad. We should at the end of our days, before sleeping, send them our thoughts and prayers so that they can continue to bear whatever difficulties they may be going through. This is what I believe anyway. Thoughts are real and can help others, I believe.

Juniper Hall is where many local children can stay with their teachers in friendly, spartan accommodation to learn about the local wildlife and the countryside. During the night, they venture out with their teachers and set traps for catching small mammals and the next day open the traps to view the mammals caught, make notes, sketch them, measure them, weigh them and then let them go again. No harm is done to the creatures at all. Mostly they catch wood mice, voles, toads, with the occasional weasel or small baby rabbit. Baby rabbits are called kittens. I shall stay there Mum says but only when I am ten. My ambition is to see or catch a Dormouse but as you know they are nocturnal and are quite elusive in the daytime. Did you know that nocturnal means that they are active at night? Well done you, if you knew this. Did you know that 'spartan' means 'lacking in comfort'?

We are finishing off our food and drinks kindly prepared by Monaie's dad when we spot an anxious-looking Bora cycling near where we have parked our blue horse truck. He looks stressed out. We, however, find it both amusing and worrying. Amusing, because he looks funny in his tight Lycra bike gear and bright pink helmet and worrying, because we wonder what on earth he is doing here.

Bora places his bicycle next to the blue horse truck and begins running up the hillside to where we are relaxing.

Amazingly, he is not completely out of breath even after running fast up our steep grassy hillside. He then says, after struggling to relieve his head of the helmet, "Princess Beatriz... I must **always** know where you are. This was agreed with your father before he agreed that you could come. I must know exactly where you are **at all times**."

"We didn't think. Sorry," Monaie's dad says.

"From now on please let me know where you are going and with whom you will be with so I am able, if necessary, to assist you and protect you." Bora is now scratching his beard with anxiety.

Princess Beatriz agrees and blushes to show that she is embarrassed by what he has said. Rob asks him to put his phone number into his phone and Bora does this.

Pete, who does not miss much then asks, "How did you know we were here then?"

"I cannot lie to you all after all you have done for Princess Beatriz and I. When I walked past the blue horse truck last night, I placed a tiny radio tracker under the wheel side. This is a highly sophisticated device that can track wherever you are and I can access my iPhone to tell me where that is. It is linked to one of our satellites."

Pete and Monaie's dad both wondered just who Bora really was. He was certainly a very good swimmer, a very fast cyclist from watching him arrive here and certainly a mystery for what little we know about him and just one of his gadgets.

Monaie's dad then said what Pete was just thinking, "I wonder just how much you have not told us."

"Princess Beatriz coming here to help her father, the Professor, to defect to this country could so easily go wrong. There was no way the Professor could trust this mission to just any man. I am a highly trained and extremely fit man who will do his best to protect Princess Beatriz, and now all of you, as best as I can. I need to know where you are going and who you are seeing from now on. Is this clear? It really is for your own protection. I promise that I will have your protection and your best interests in mind at all times."

"Yes," we all replied together. We were beginning to understand just how important Bora was to our health and to our safety.

Then Monaie stood up to attract some attention and said loudly, "Yes," and we all broke down into uncontrollable laughter.

"You see... the North Kortanese will have spies in your country," he continued in a very low voice as though he could be picked up here by North Kortana, "...that they can ask to check out anything and at any time. Distance is no object to them. Again, they are highly trained men or women who will do everything to please the Leader of North Kortana. If they know Princess Beatriz is here, they will do everything to find her and take her back before she can obtain asylum but she can only do that when her father arrives here in about seven days. I have already given the go-ahead for the Professor to leave but once he does they will try to find him, the submarine and Princess Beatriz. Once they know the submarine has finally left North Kortana again and this time with the Professor, they will want to try to trace it to wherever it has gone. They will do everything that they can to locate the submarine and the Professor. They will not hesitate to order his death in the event that they decide it is in their own best interests to kill him. The last thing they want is for him to defect and give up all what he knows to the United Kingdom."

We sat on the short grass and tried to take it all in. I just thought to myself that we were all just kids and maybe we had taken on too much in spite of how much we cared for the Princess; the girl with a parrot.

From now on, we had to be most careful, that was for sure. Monaie's dad offered Bora a lift which he accepted and so Bora ended up in the back of the truck with his bicycle, Pete and Rob. The last we heard before we arrived home at Sloping Meadow was Bora and the boys trying to whistle the same song in tune. My own view was that they failed. It sounded bad. No doubt the boys and Bora would disagree with this analysis.

Aren't boys crazy?

Chapter 8
Sir John Soane's Museum WC2

Sir John Soane was a famous architect and explorer, who collected many antiques and artefacts from all over the world and lived in Lincoln's Inn Fields, near Holborn, London, where he placed his massive collection of paintings, drawings and artefacts so that friends and other people may view them.

Today it is a wonderful, free museum in Lincoln's Inn Fields, where every child over the age of seven should be taken by their parents to marvel at just how many wonderful things are gathered into one beautiful home. Ask your parents or your guardians or even your teachers to take you there and all of you will enjoy it and, on the way home you may, if you wish, visit St Bride's Church.

On your way out of the Sir John Soane's Museum please try to put some money in the collection box to help preserve the museum for other children and other grown-ups to view.

It was Pete's idea, and after making sure he had texted Bora so he knew where we were going, we all bought our tickets at Kershalton Beeches Station and headed for Clapham Junction Railway Station, the busiest station in the world apparently, to change for a train to Waterloo, then by foot over the delightful Waterloo Bridge, with great views across the Thames, as well as great views of some very famous landmarks. Once on Waterloo Bridge, we can see Big Ben and the Houses of Parliament and we can see the National Theatre. Try and see this great modern building at night if you can, as it is lit up with colours. I like it lit in shades of theatre red; it looks stunning. Mum and Dad took me there once.

We walk down the Strand area and up the road until we bear right then turn right into the very famous Lincoln's Inn Fields. Mum says you could get attacked here a long time ago as it was open fields at one time, before the government at the time deliberately decided to build the Royal Courts of Justice nearby to keep levels of crime down. This had the immediate effect of reducing crime in the area many years ago. Today many famous barristers and solicitors and judges may be seen walking around during their lunch breaks, taking the air and checking their texts and enjoying the gardens attached to Lincoln's Inn. Try not to tell anyone but these judges' gardens are beautiful and just what the judiciary and those working hard in the courts need to find peace before dealing with all the many strands of justice.

Just up the north side of Lincoln's Inn you can find The Sir John Soane's Museum. Check the opening times, as my mum did, but we were allowed in at eleven a.m. on a Thursday morning, exactly two days after we were visited on the River Bede by a princess. A princess who wishes us to treat her as a non-princess. We all keep curtsying then laughing when we realise that she does not need this whilst staying with us at Sloping Meadow.

We stroll in and I should have explained that we are without Monaie and her dad but we will meet them later on in Sloping Meadow as Princess Beatriz has not yet fully seen it in daylight.

Inside this museum, Rob and Pete are immediately enthralled by the wonderful things to see. Great paintings and statues immediately hit you with their majesty and spectacle. Some of these paintings are stored in large thin cases that open out for you to flick through them like massive magazine racks. These must be some six feet high. The steep staircases are awesome as well but what really stuns us all is just how many different items are put together here in this one home. What a magnificent home Sir John had and what a marvellous collection. He travelled a lot around the world and collected many diverse things that he liked. They are all here to be seen, some of which date back thousands of years to Ancient Egypt and to the times of the great pharaohs, who believed in strange gods that took the shape of crocodiles or wolves or hyenas and even birds.

How cool were the Ancient Egyptians?

Chapter 9
North Kortana – Pagyang – Local Time: Five p.m.

Breaking News:

Word is officially out that one of our chief professors has gone missing. He was last seen today at three p.m. but since he was requested by the military to report for duty, he has failed to do so. This makes it a high-profile matter.

He is Professor Sebastian Mendoza and so that you may help our esteemed beloved leader locate him, here is his photograph. This is urgent. He is absent without permission.

Please share this photograph around North Kortana so we can all help search for him. He is working on some very important scientific research so please tell any member of the establishment or the police forces if you come across him. We must find him urgently. He may need our support and help.

This is the message that has just gone out on North Kortanese Television, read by a middle-aged and almost hysterical woman. Her voice it is that amplifies the hysteria, as it is shrill and fast.

Meanwhile, Professor Sebastian Mendoza is currently safe in the very warm and comfortable Nuclear Submarine that he has helped design. It runs like clockwork and the journey is as pleasant as it can be, apart from the constant, deafening hum of the Nuclear Engines. He has wonderful meals prepared by the chef on board and this time he has six loyal crew to help him, should he need help. They will rest in shifts and get him to the River Bede in England as soon as they can to join his daughter, Princess Beatriz. If required they will die for him; they are that loyal to him.

ETA, Estimated Time of Arrival, is Friday eight p.m.

Unfortunately for them, the Supreme Leader has ordered satellite tracing to take place over the last forty-eight hours for all submarines that have left the North Kortanese area and this means that they have been able to calculate that the Nuclear Submarine on which Princess Beatriz was brought to London on has now been easily traced to the River Bede in England. They are that sophisticated with their technology.

Everything leaves its own trace on this world. Mum has told me that every time we touch anything we deposit our DNA, basically these are small particles that only belong to us and can be traced back to us. How amazing is that? Every person ever born has, for example, their own individual fingerprint. Isn't that incredible? When you are seated near a window that has condensation on it, you can see your own fingerprint if you gently place your finger or thumb on the condensation that has formed on the glass of the window. Check it out. Or, with your mum's permission, dip your finger end in paint or ink and place it on some white paper and you will see your own individual fingerprint that only you possess. Trust me.

And worse still, all communications between the River Bede and external callers, and that includes phone calls, as well as mobile phone calls, have been traced and configured, and sometimes even tri-angulated, leading the North Kortanese to have pin-pointed that one of those still active phones traced, lies in the building known as Sir John Soane's Museum, London, England, just off Lincoln's Inn Fields. This is, unfortunately for us, where we currently are.

Immediately, North Kortana activates their number one spy living in London. She is currently attached to a hairdresser in Bond Street and if you saw her you would not know that she was very skilled and highly trained as a North Kortanese Spy. You may just think that she was as she seems; a bored hairdresser constantly using her iPhone.

She is a woman of thirty-six and her name is Hye Booh. Just so you know 'Hye' means in Kortanese 'Intelligent Woman'. She definitely lives up to her name.

In London, it is now eleven twenty a.m. as Hye Booh arrives at Holborn readying herself to enter the Sir John Soane's Museum. She is armed and she is dangerous. She has minutes earlier located her weapon of choice hidden inside a litter bin in Lincoln's Inn Fields (placed there by an associate) and now has it primed and ready to discharge in the event she needs to. She is the best marksperson from North Kortana in the UK at this moment in time. There are many reasons to fear her; especially if you know the whereabouts of a certain princess.

Hye Booh is expecting anything unusual but not, thankfully, children. She carefully places by the door a tiny camera to capture the images of every single person who enters or leaves the Sir John Soane's Museum. Hers is the first image captured by that tiny camera so you can now see from that image what she looks like as she enters the museum that morning; not knowing what to look for but knowing that she must expect the unexpected. She is very alert. She is constantly in touch with contacts in North London, who are, in turn, constantly being updated by North Kortana by satellite.

Since she was chosen at eighteen, she has trained hard to serve the Glorious Leader. She has qualified only four years ago as a spy for North Kortana and her reputation is of being ruthless and super intelligent. She works in London and keeps herself to herself until she is needed to be activated. Her last assignment was three months ago so she is keen to show how her training and fitness since then has made her even sharper and even more full of energy. She is dynamic.

It is Princess Beatriz who felt unease when she first sees Hye Booh arrive at the foot of the stairs. Hye Booh, once activated, has this energy that radiates great power due to her intensive training, so immediately Princess Beatriz covers her face with a long scarf just in time. You and I might call this female intuition. Hye Booh has very intense hazel eyes that look scary when you see them through her sunglasses. Have a look at her photograph. Can you see her eyes? Her eyes look cold and calculating to me. What do you think?

Thank god Princess Beatriz has covered her face because within seconds of this action by her, Hye Booh is scrutinising carefully every single face that she now encounters. She then comes noiselessly up one floor on the beautiful staircase and scrutinises Princess Beatriz's face looking intently for any slight signs of stress or nerves or fear. There are none. Princess Beatriz is in her princess mode and will act cool and calm under pressure. Her dad taught her how to keep cool under pressure when she was younger and when he was physically well.

She confides in me that she wonders just who the woman is who has just entered the building. I think, *Oh my god,* trying to keep cool. The slim woman looks extremely fit and totally vigilant.

My own instinct, which Mum always tells me to listen to, now clearly tells me that I have to be very careful around this new woman who has silently entered our world here.

It really will be only a matter of hours before it will be known that Princess Beatriz is in London. This will be verified once the uncovered face of the Princess is seen on leaving the museum; when all the photos captured on the tiny camera are processed. We are not aware of this because we are so unsuspecting but then on the positive side we do have Bora and at least Bora knows this time where we are, but where is he?

We walk into one Egyptian room and there are many sarcophagi in it. You may know already that these are long coffin-like boxes that house the Egyptian Mummies to keep them safe until they are able to make it to the afterlife. It is a way of further protecting their mummified bodies from decay and robbery by tomb robbers and covering them respectfully to help them make the journey to the Underworld, as the

Egyptians believed in a life after death, where strangely they believed they could still utilise their possessions such as chairs, musical instruments or even their weapons of war or chariots in the next world.

Claire, Pete, Rob, Beatriz and I are the only ones in the room and nearly jump out of our skins when suddenly one of these empty sarcophagi, or coffins, opens slowly, revealing Bora, lying down and smiling, telling us,

"Ha. The woman in the shades is a Kortanese spy. I saw her enter the building and hid in here hoping you would come in. Her name is Hye Booh. She is not sure who you are Princess Beatriz, yet, but when she is, she will try to either capture or destroy you. We have to leave as soon as we can. What I suggest is that Pete and Rob walk, with you in the middle, and then hurry out to the field opposite where I will meet you under the rain shelter adjacent to where netball is being played by adults. Go now quickly. The rest can follow me but make out I am your teacher telling you off then shouting at you to leave so expect me to be loud when telling you off. Just grab Giselle and get her to follow us out."

We rush out and in no time at all Bora spots the tiny camera clicking silently at us as we leave. He is still doing a great impression of being our schoolteacher telling us off. There is no time for him to crush the camera with his fists so we all move fast to get out into the summer heat of Lincoln's Inn Fields. He is aware more than us that we are in danger now, because Hye Booh will know from the photos once processed from her phone who he is and, even if she does not, those in North Korea will, when the photos are transmitted there, from her iPhone via satellite.

At the rain shelter we spot Pete, Rob and Princess Beatriz and Bora instructs us now to be aware that we are in very serious danger. I ask why and he replies that we are because they will soon know that Princess Beatriz has run away to England and is being helped by him and that Professor Mendoza is on his way to meet her. Hye Booh, he explains, will not hesitate to kill us all. Her training will not permit her to show any mercy to any of us.

He directs us to run down the side streets until we come to the back of the Royal Courts of Justice where he is convinced he may be able to lose Hye Booh as he says he knows the layout of the building that Mum says was designed by a man who always dreamed of designing a cathedral but Mum believes he succeeded with the Royal Courts of Justice as it looks either just like a beautiful Fairy Tale Castle (my view) or a wonderful Cathedral (Mum's view). I personally think the Royal Courts of Justice looks **exactly** like a Fairy Tale Castle. Try and visit it if you are able to. From the outside it looks beautiful.

As I turn the corner, I notice Hye Booh running fast from the rain shelter towards us, still on her iPhone. I can't tell a lie now, I feel fear. I have fear for Princess Beatriz and fear for all of us. We run faster because of the fear. My heart is beating fast inside my running body.

I am convinced everyone that I pass can hear my beating heart. I expect all those I pass by to wonder what the loud noise is. My heart feels bigger than before and so noisy. I can actually feel my blood pumping fast around my veins and especially inside my ears. I am breathing much heavier and feel stronger and lighter. This is caused by adrenaline, Mum says, a hormone being released directly into our bloodstreams when we need extra strength to run away or to fight. It makes me feel slightly strange and slightly sick. For me though it is much better to know what it is than to worry about it because I do not know.

We all run together not sure just how the future will turn out.

Who knows?

Chapter 10
The Bear Garden

We quickly enter the back entrance of the Royal Courts of Justice. Bora is still pretending to be our school teacher and says in front of the security guards, who we now face before we are permitted to enter,

"Come on you lot. We have time just to look at the Judges' Exhibition in the Grand Hall then we must go, if we are to see St Paul's Cathedral today."

The security guards let us all in, briefly asking only Bora to put his things in a tray, like in airports, which they then scan.

Just behind us we all notice Hye Booh being asked to place personal items in a tray so they can be scanned. She must have hidden her weapon somewhere because it does not come up on the scanning machine. What she has done is place it high enough for it not to have been detected and rather deftly collects it again as she turns back from collecting her items scanned. The security guards do not notice anything, only her wonderful smile that they return to her, transfixed by her smart, slim body and those captivating, hazel eyes. She has mesmerised them with her charisma. Even I am mesmerised by her charisma. I suspect, Bora is, also. It does not lessen the danger we are in, however. We must keep our wits about us now or we will most certainly be killed.

We then race ahead having got the all clear from the guards a few minutes before she has.

"Follow me tightly," Bora says and he runs through the main hall and past the Judges' Exhibition (basically comprising a history of what judges wore) and straight up some very grand stone staircase that is quite near the Strand side and then runs even faster. He is as fit as we thought he was; he is, once again, not out of breath. At the top of the stone stairs he tells us, in a low clear voice,

"You are now in the Bear Garden. When no one is looking, do exactly what I do."

He then opens a door to a stone balcony outside that faces the main Strand with all the traffic going by below and he disappears behind the smallish wall. He is virtually unseen from the inside as well as from the outside once he gets down low.

We all copy and as soon as we do, we shut the door leading to the open balcony and, believe it or not, we are no longer visible to anyone coming into the Bear Garden and passing the door to the balcony.

The Bear Garden is really a large and wonderful room about one hundred and forty years old, used now by solicitors or barristers or their clerks to discuss cases they are acting in with their clients or to check from the Daily List which courts that they are due to appear in for their clients and at what time.

We now hear Hye Booh in the Bear Garden on her phone speaking to someone in Kortanese right next to us but we are really on the outside of the wall she is walking by. Never in a thousand years would she have thought that we were right next to her but on the very outside of the stone balcony, feeling the hot sun on our necks, crouched down low. We are literally inches away from her and her automatic gun. Only the thickness of the wall separates us from death.

We again hear her speaking into her phone and walking away from us, towards the Queen's Bench Division, which is on the same floor and we turn back through the door of the balcony and escape back down the stone staircase with Bora, the very last one to leave.

We now find ourselves out in the Strand and are hit by the heavy smell of the pollution from the many vehicles passing us in both directions and cross at the Cenotaph, which is a monument that commemorates those that gave their lives in all the wars. Bora leads us now to the left, running down towards a very famous church, St Bride's, in the Strand. This church, designed by Sir Christopher Wren, is special because people all over the world copy its design for their multi-tiered wedding cakes. I only know this because Mum told me this. I wish Mum was with me now as I am beginning to feel scared for Pete, and my friends and even for Bora.

As we go in this wedding cake church, we realise that there is a recital of classical music taking place, possibly from the composer, Bach, Bora thinks, but we head down some wooden stairs on the left side to what is a small exhibition showing parts of a very old Roman Wall found there and we are safe, for at least the time being.

The music of Bach fills our ears from the large church organ above. All of us feel the vibrations of the sound of the organ playing through the walls and the floor. Each one of us feels the vibrations in our tummies. We smile more in relief than anything else and we all think privately that we are pleased to have Bora on our side. The music is really very uplifting and we all feel like heroes and heroines when it reaches our ears and inspires us.

When we finally leave at about one p.m. we are hungry and the rain has started. The rain in London always seems to me to be grey and a depressing grey at that. Then we travel down some back streets and down some very old stone stairs and end up coming up the right side of the River Thames of Waterloo Bridge, facing Westminster. We take the stone steps up to the top of the bridge. We cross the bridge again to Waterloo Station side and then make our way to Clapham Junction changing there for Kershalton Beeches Station and home.

We did not even stop for a bite to eat but are glad to see Sloping Meadow and Monaie and her father. He valiantly prepares a meal for us. Beef Burgers and chips. How healthy is that?

After this late lunch, we then formally introduce Benjamin the donkey to Princess Beatriz and she strokes him and then rushes upstairs to feed her hungry parrot with food brought in her long case from her home. She loves Benjamin,

Monaie's donkey, she tells us, and glows every time she meets him.

We are exhausted but happy to be alive. We show Princess Beatriz Sloping Meadow just after the drizzling rain has finished and she loves it. Certainly, it looks fresh and shiny as the sun glints on wet cobbles forming some of the paths and also on the rims of flowers holding tiny raindrops.

I think to myself, *What have we agreed to? Things are definitely becoming very serious now.*

It strikes me now that we need to be brave in what is an unknown future.

I really hope that everything can work out for the Princess and for her father; my very next hope is that everything works out for all of us as well.

Can you blame me for thinking this way?

Mum says you must look after your body as you only have one. All of us are in danger, it seems to me.

Chapter 11
A Drone Appears, Then Disappears

From her iPhone Princess Beatriz sends Pete a photo of a painting that her father, Professor Sebastian Mendoza, says is worth a lot of money and that he hopes to bring with him on the submarine. She tells us it is a very old painting depicting a Maya scene from long ago and which his grandfather was given many years ago by relatives living in Mexico, who later travelled to Peru. There are still Mayan people living today who are descendants from those living hundreds of years ago and who used to sacrifice their enemies to their gods by decapitating them and rolling their heads and bodies down the sides of the great pyramids in the ancient Mayan cities, built deep in the forests of Mexico.

The modern-day Mayans are very small in stature compared to the rest of the world's peoples but they are a wonderful race of people and are very friendly nowadays towards anyone visiting them. The painting shows a Mayan boy dressed as one of the old gods near the base of one of the many pyramids in the area of Chichen-Itza which today can be found near Cancun, Mexico. In your lifetime please try and visit Chichen-Itza as it is well worth seeing the marvellous pyramid there.

Here is the photo of the painting so you can see it. We just all hope the Professor can safely arrive on Friday at eight p.m.

We all admire the photo of the painting and all look forward very much to seeing the Professor on Friday now, with or without the painting.

Sloping Meadow now proudly displays marvellous summer flowers that can take your breath away as they are so delightful. There are pink Sweet Williams that look resplendent. There are also the large Michaelmas Daisies that are scattered among the tall grasses of the meadow competing with the tall Sun Flowers looking like mini suns covered in orange and deep yellow petals. In the damper, wetter parts of Sloping Meadow are tall green ornamental wild grasses that have silver and brown heads and wild thistles with purple and brown heads covered in what I call 'whiskers of white fur'. Every so often the light breezes disturb these white whiskers, forcing them to take flight high in the swirling currents of warmer air. In and out of the lower bushes, called purple Berberis, I can see tiny Wrens flitting about with great skill to avoid the prickles of the bushes. I point these tiny birds out to the Princess.

We are then fortunate to see my favourite bird, a Jay. It seems to be jumping up and down possibly trying to attract worms up from the ground which will presumably come up believing the sounds the Jay is creating to be raindrops. If you patter the grass with both your hands, you will find that worms will rise to the surface as they love it when it rains. Try it and see how many worms appear if you manage to duplicate the sounds of rain falling. Pete and I have done this many times with great success in Sloping Meadow.

Princess Beatriz is suitably impressed with all that Sloping Meadow has to offer. She has never seen wild Magpies before and now finds them amusing to watch. They are always after something. They will steal from your jewellery boxes if you leave your bedroom windows open in summer, as they find shiny objects irresistible. The smell of the wild roses in the meadow is overwhelming. A sweet heady fragrance capturing all the essence of a hot summer's day in one floral scent.

Although it seems all greens and yellows and light browns, on closer inspection we see that the greens for example are, in fact, many different hues. In fact, we have not properly realised before that there are possibly dozens of different shades of green in this one meadow. Closer inspection reveals that this really is the case here.

There are some marshy patches, Monaie's dad tells us, that contain natural springs here. They are presumably called springs because the water literally springs up and overflows. They can be drunk, he assures us "as the water has travelled over many fine granite rocks absorbing rich minerals that are beneficial to health".

Suddenly, Rob shouts over to us all,

"Here is a natural spring. Anyone fancy a drink?"

"Yes please," Claire responds rapidly, bending right down and seeing the natural spring spurting out between moss-coloured rocks as a thick flow of water. She drinks from it.

"Wow!" she exclaims, "This has a really great taste to it."

The water itself is very cold having travelled a long way across and through stretches of underground rocks and carries with it many traces of minerals that are good for animals and humans to imbibe.

We take it in turns to satisfy our thirsts and we all agree with Claire's description of the quality.

"That is the first time that I have drunk from a real natural spring," Princess Beatriz declares.

A beautiful cerulean blue sky covers us now in Sloping Meadow. There are no clouds; just pure English sunshine.

Princess Beatriz, on gazing up, after her drink, spots it first.

Shiny and bright and also metallic in medium. The Princess points at it.

"Drone above us," Pete states.

"Sure looks like a drone but it has something on it," Rob says.

Giselle, who has been staring hard at it, suddenly states,

"A camera! The drone is going to film us! They'll know the Princess is here with us! Quick, everyone hide under the Douglas Firs."

We run. We hide.

The drone carries on and then circles the area but heads off towards Stratton Common area.

"Wait until we let Bora know."

From the air a helicopter is now making a lot of noise well above us but it has seen us and lands, blasting the air around us and flattening the long meadow grasses. The sounds of the rotors both deafen and hurt our ears. We are unsure just how friendly this helicopter will prove to be but then a mechanical voice comes out from a megaphone being held by a lady in the passenger side of the helicopter.

"**LUCY**. We work for the UK Government and are friends. **DO NOT BE ALARMED!** We were following the drone picked up on radar by the RAF, the Royal Air Force, flying past Southampton."

The engine is cut suddenly and a woman climbs out just as soon as the rotating blades of the helicopter have stopped moving. She is taking off what looks to me like a leather flying jacket. She crosses over to us and stands in just a blue shirt in the full sunshine of Sloping Meadow. Her shirt mimics the sky's colour. There is a strong smell of aviation fuel now all around us and all over Sloping Meadow.

"Good afternoon. My name is Helen Scott and I am a British Agent currently attached to the UK Borders Unit, Home Office. We have been told about you all by Bora."

We all stare gobsmacked.

The pilot of the helicopter pulls his helmet and earphones off, unzips his thick leather flying jacket and utters, to our astonishment,

"Yes, I told them about you."

We are amazed.

It is indeed Bora.

Giselle is happy to see him and smiles at him. He returns her smile with genuine warmth.

"We are fearful that the drone may have had a small missile on board intent on destroying you all so we followed it as soon as the RAF had spotted it on their radar screens. I am obliged to my friends in the UK for hearing my story and believing me, and providing me with the use of their helicopter," he continues.

Giselle says, "Bora, it is so good to see you. What will happen to the drone now?"

Helen Scott then said, "Can you still see it now?"

"Yes," Claire says.

"Well," Helen says, "can you now see the very small red plane coming into view from the west?"

"Yes," we all say together, looking towards the west.

"Well, now watch their drone closely."

About five seconds later the red plane fires a small shiny missile at the drone which turns into a fireball and explodes with black smoke only left in the sky where it once was. The black smoke slowly dissipates. We can only see vast expanses of cerulean blue sky appearing now and nothing else.

"I have ordered the RAF to shoot it down," Helen coolly states.

Pete steps forward and takes a photo of Helen so you can see it. She immediately orders him to delete it which he does, after he lets you see it.

How cool is she? Just the sort of woman who makes females everywhere feel great about what they may achieve in life. Here she is in Pete's photo.

Please may I ask you **not to share this photo with anyone** as her position as a UK British Agent will be compromised. Also, I will be in serious trouble.

Helen Scott looks to me about thirty and is glowing with good health. Like Hye Booh, she looks alert and ready for action. I think it important to have female role models to look up to. Someone once said to me that if we really believe in something, then it really can happen for us and will definitely happen.

I believe that it was my mum who said this. Here is a photo of my mum to remind you what she looks like. She is my number one role model, but Helen has also impressed me in a short time frame. I believe that every girl and boy needs a role model, someone to look up to and emulate. It is good practice to think, when you have problems in life, now what would Mum do in this situation or what would my role model do or say in these circumstances. It can only help I am sure.

No one need suffer alone. There are always people around to ask for help if you find difficulties in living or knowing how to behave in any circumstances. We all need help and support in this life and I believe that we should always consider asking for help from a teacher or from someone we trust when we need to. Mum says there is no need to keep things that are worrying you to yourself.

Oh and I believe that it is true that there is nothing that you can experience or feel in this lifetime that has not already been experienced or felt by someone else before you.

It is so easy to ask for help so you may as well do so. What do you think?

Is Mum correct?

Chapter 12
Promises and Threats

There is no way I shall be able to describe in detail just exactly what Helen Scott's personality is like. It is forbidden by MI6 to whom she belongs. All I can say is that the boys thought she looked great and the girls thought she was great. Two very different perspectives, I can assure you. Basically, the boys soon became very fond of her largely because of her looks, while the girls, being far more sensible anyway than boys, we very quickly saw her as a role model. She was someone we could emulate and imitate.

She quickly had a rapport with all of us, especially the females. The girls were very pleased to have her in our company not only because she would protect us but also because she inspired us with her confidence in her own abilities. Only my mum inspires me as much as Helen.

Bora tells us that because of the situation with the North Kortanese knowing that the Nuclear Submarine came up the Thames and into the River Bede, we now need protection from the UK's MI6 and hence we have Helen Scott, an Agent from MI6, as well as Bora, a Secret Agent from South Kortana. I think we will need both of them.

They ask us to sit down in Monaie's lounge and they both wish to make it clear,

"We wish to make it clear," Helen starts, "that we are both here to protect you. We **promise** that we will protect you with our lives until Professor Mendoza arrives and we can arrange for him and Princess Beatriz, his daughter, to seek out asylum in the UK. Once that happens they will be moved to a safe house and our job will be over. We have licences to carry guns and that is what we both do now, carry guns, because the North Kortanese will not hesitate to do all they can to despatch you all. Before any of you ask, despatch means kill. We promise that we will do the opposite and protect you all."

Monaie's dad makes us all tea and biscuits. He is a rock!

Bora tells us all to enjoy the rest of the afternoon because tonight we are being treated to a great show, 'The Lion King' at The Lyceum, thanks to MI6, who are keen to acknowledge that we are helping them to find out more about North Kortana.

Helen tells us that she alone will accompany us to The Lyceum Theatre in the Strand, London, as Bora has to make preparations for the Nuclear Submarine to alter its destination to the River Thames, South Bank. A decision has been made to pick Professor Mendoza tonight at eight p.m. at the South Bank, right near to the Globe Theatre, as it will be so open that it is unlikely the North Kortanese will suspect it as a chosen place for the Professor to leave the Nuclear Submarine. The Metropolitan Police will be informed shortly before the submarine arrives not to intercept anyone arriving on the submarine and not to get involved in case there is a gun battle. It largely depends of course on whether the North Kortanese are instructed to take the Professor alive, which is what the authorities are now thinking as likely. Apparently, North Kortana cannot afford to lose their best Nuclear Scientist. Not at this stage of the game anyway.

The idea is that once the Professor arrives and is helped by Bora from the submarine, he will go straight to the Lyceum Theatre where he will be surrounded by theatre goers making it an unlikely place for the North Kortanese to cause an international scene by having a gun fight there with MI6 and Bora. Additionally, all those theatre goers with their iPhones, could record it all which is not what the North Kortanese would wish for.

"What is in our favour," Bora explains, "is that the North Kortanese may expect the submarine to let the Professor out on the River Bede tomorrow night, but in fact it will be the South Bank tonight, right by the Globe Theatre. It has meant that the Nuclear Submarine has been travelling at maximum speed for the last few hours and should make the new rendezvous at eight p.m. tonight."

"Cool," says Claire, excited by the thought of seeing 'The Lion King' tonight.

"Cool, but very dangerous," Bora says, "because I cannot tell you who, in the passing crowd, is just a tourist, visitor or spy intent on harming you."

Bora kisses Helen politely on both her cheeks and announces, "I am leaving. Safe journey to the theatre. Will see you later, Helen, in the Lyceum Theatre with Professor Mendoza."

"Yes," is all she says and turns to us and asks, "Can any of you play table tennis then?"

Bora goes and we end up playing table tennis until it is time to get ready. Pete tells our parents that we are going to see 'The Lion King' as Monaie's dad has six free tickets and can they tell all the other parents please. There are of course seven tickets because our MI6 Officer, Helen Scott, is also coming with us to help ensure that we are safe. Monaie is tired now at seven p.m. so will go to bed soon. When she is older, of course she will be given the opportunity to also enjoy 'The Lion King'.

The table tennis has given us an appetite and so we are treated by the MI6 Officer to fried chicken and French fries. How cool is that?

Helen can see we are ready so she sits us down before we leave and says,

"Tonight is a very important night in your lives not least because it is also a very important night for your country. By safely pulling Professor Mendoza from the Nuclear Submarine Bora will be helping your country to know vital information about the secret state of North Kortana and its strange leader. The information can be shared with all those countries that believe in democracy and decency. In turn, of course we will also be in a position to help North Kortana, as the ordinary people, who are largely innocent of these state crimes, can then be helped to see the ridiculous views that the leader holds about Nuclear Bombs."

She tells us that the offices where they work at the MI6 Building on the railway line to Waterloo has received a communication from North Kortana that threatens London with terrible consequences unless we hand Professor Mendoza over on his arrival.

"We shall of course do everything we can to help him defect to London and shall ignore the threat from North Kortana." Helen informs.

She then adds, just before we leave,

"Oh, by the way, we shall be travelling tonight to the Strand in style."

She smiles and as she does, her nose and her face crease with laughter lines.

"In style?" I ask, suspiciously.

"Yes, Lucy, in the blue horse truck and I shall be driving. Monaie and her father will remain here until hopefully, we see them again."

"Oh, My God!" we say, pulling faces, as we know that it is hardly in style. It will be, as it always is, a very bumpy and uncomfortable ride, made better only by the fact that Helen is with us driving us and protecting us.

"Look," Helen responds, "the North Kortanese will surely not suspect an old blue horse truck and, in any event, we are in London with many friends who we can call on, should the need arise, trust me."

"We are in your hands," Claire says and asks Princess Beatriz if she can sit next to her and the Princess agrees with a smile. Princess Beatriz and Claire are hitting it off.

It takes Helen a few goes on the truck's gears to get the hang of them but her training kicks in well and soon we are being driven away relatively smoothly, with Rob and Pete in the back and Helen, Claire, Princess Beatriz, Giselle and I in the long front seat. Hardly really comfortable but worse for the two boys in the back. Our boys are not fussy.

Helen has dressed up for the theatre and is wearing a black trouser suit and high heels. She looks great according to the boys and elegant according to the rest of us. She is wearing a small diamond on a silver chain and to me she looks like a princess herself. We all think she has a lovely personality and I think we will all fight to sit next to her in the theatre.

We have left Kershalton Village a while ago now and we move across the Southeast of London northwards to Morden where we will drive up to the Waterloo area, through Wimbledon.

On Waterloo Bridge, Helen is stopped by a policeman and someone standing next to the policeman then squirts a cold spray straight through the passenger side window that we have partially opened for air.

Immediately, we fall fast asleep. Helen, who is struggling to breath, also falls asleep now.

In the back of the blue horse truck Pete sends one text message before the back door of the truck is opened and the same cold spray is squirted all over the boys.

Helen is pushed over to one side and a new driver gets in and drives away like a fanatic, doing a left at the end of Waterloo Bridge and circles away towards Nelson's Column then turns in the middle of the road and heads again eastwards towards St Paul's Cathedral.

Pete's text message is to Bora.

When Bora opens it, it reads:

'On Waterloo Bridge. Stopped by policeman but he has no number on shoulder. Think possibly North Kortanese. Help us.'

Chapter 13
Stratford, East London

Pete and Rob wake up first, then the rest of us.

Helen is alive and well, but tied up, as we are.

We are not gagged over our mouths and find that we can still see and hear.

We are in a room. A dirty, cold and grey room with no light. A smell of dampness and neglect fills the room. Dirty clothes litter the floor.

Helen miraculously manages to stand up using all her strength in her legs and sees the blue horse truck outside on a road that says Vernon Road E15.

She knows immediately that she is in Stratford, East London, in a residential road, inside someone's terraced house. She then collapses with the effort of moving in the tight ropes that hold her arms and legs. The toxic spray has weakened not only her but all of us.

At least all of us are currently unharmed and able to breathe. We do have headaches though but that is all. Probably caused by the spray used on us.

"God knows what that spray was, Lucy, but it was very effective," Helen mutters to me who is next to her. "It's certainly new to me."

We then notice, on looking at each other, that our eyes look sore and reddened with the gas.

Helen is quick to say to us all, "We do not know how long we are going to be held here so just keep calm. Remember that Bora has placed a satellite tracer on the blue horse truck so he will know where we are but he may not think we are lost yet."

"He knows we have been stopped on Waterloo Bridge by a suspicious-looking policeman," Pete says.

"How?" enquires Helen.

"Because when I heard the policeman ask you to stop, I looked through a side crack and saw that he was not showing a police number on his shoulder so I knew he was suspicious and sent Bora a text."

"You are brilliant, Pete," Helen cried out, "Well done, you! Definitely MI6 material!"

"Thanks," Pete says and blushes.

"Well, in that case what I think is that Bora will have asked MI6 to look at this house and plan an attack on this place to free us. I must warn you that if the Special Air Service, SAS, come in they are very noisy with grenades that go off. These are stun grenades so will not harm us but hopefully stun the North Kortanese. Do not be afraid. I am with you."

We waited and waited on the SAS and then we waited.

Nothing.

Until eight p.m. precisely.

Then we hear a great **BANG!** followed by another **BANG!** The flashes that come with the two bangs blind us with their brightness for a whole minute. A white smoke fills the room now following the flashes.

We cheer and then four SAS men burst in and all carry high-powered rifles with torch lights affixed to them, pointing at us and shouting,

"UP AND OUT NOW! UP AND OUT NOW!"

We struggle, as had Helen before us, to stand but the SAS officers then push us up and force us out into the hallway and out into the road.

Helen screams at them, **"MI6 Officer on Duty: Helen Scott."**

"We know! We know!" they shout back.

They free Helen and will not touch us until they check us all for any explosives that may have been tied to us.

When Helen tells them we are with her, they undo our ropes and order us to the side of the blue horse truck.

When the SAS men open the back of the truck, bullets begin flying around as three North Kortanese Agents are inside and open fire.

The SAS return rapid fire and destroy all three instantly.

"No sign of Hye Booh, then?" Helen shouts.

"None, madam," the SAS reply. I then realise that every one of these SAS men are covered in black makeup presumably to disguise their identities.

We are glad to get out of there and we are then placed into a police truck and taken to the Lyceum Theatre, having missed only the very beginning of 'The Lion King'.

We think, at that time, that our troubles are now over but little did we know, they are, in fact, just beginning.

We enjoy 'The Lion King' and then, during the interval, we are given ice cream tubs in the bar by Helen and introduced to Professor Sebastian Mendoza who carries what appears to be a painting wrapped in brown paper under his arm. While we were being rescued by the SAS, the Professor was arriving in the submarine in the South Bank of the Thames right near to where the Globe Theatre is situated. He looks just like his photo.

Princess Beatriz jumps straight into his arms and kisses and hugs him for ages.

"Papa! It really is you after all this time!"

He says, "Beatriz, I am delighted that so many friends in London have helped you and it will be great to finally apply to the UK Government for asylum, so I can defect to London."

"Please introduce me to your new friends," the Professor implores her.

"This is Lucy. This is Giselle. Oh, and this is Helen. And this is Claire. And now the boys: this is Pete and this one is Rob."

"Well, I am honoured to meet you all and please may I thank you for all your help in this matter. We must make our way to meet the officials who will organise Beatriz and I to live in this country from now on. We only have a short trip to make to Whitehall and then we can all say our fond farewells to you all. Once we are in a safe house, we will hopefully invite you to come and visit us."

I noticed that he had some sort of a cough and suddenly remembered that this was not a man in the prime of health but a man who was sick. After what seems to me to be a coughing fit, I notice what appears to me to be blood smeared on his lips. He cannot be a well man.

That 'short trip' to Whitehall will come to haunt me for a long time to come.

You will soon know why.

Chapter 14
Not Quite There Yet

We travel in a long, dark car with seven passenger seats and darkened windows and all of us are in it including Bora and our driver. We feel very special indeed.

The other car that we intend to follow to Whitehall holds Princess Beatriz, Professor Sebastian Mendoza and Helen Scott and their driver.

Both cars are bombproof, according to my brother, Pete, who seems to be living up to his new image of being a possible future MI6 agent.

Oh, the journey begins very calmly and all seems well, until what can only be described as a huge banging sound, followed immediately by a burst water main suddenly erupting in front of both cars, causing us to swerve violently and stop. We can see nothing through the darkened windows except water and lots of it. It is like being in a massive car wash. The pressure from the burst water main has sent the water up very high into the air; it now cascades down everywhere. We appear to be inside a ceaseless waterfall. Our visibility is compromised.

In the mix-up, both drivers are somehow swapped for North Kortanese and the poor original drivers are thrown out onto the hard London road. There was nothing they could do as the element of surprise was just too much and just too shocking. Water is now everywhere.

Bora was going to react but the new driver is heavily armed and can seemingly drive one-handed, whilst holding his automatic weapon on his lap, with a finger on its trigger, ready to fire at Bora, or indeed any one of us.

The same situation was going on with Helen's car containing the Professor, Princess Beatriz and herself.

We just have to sit tight and see what might happen and if an opportunity might arise to escape with our lives. Who knows what these people are capable of?

Bora intones, "Keep calm. We will not be harmed by them."

Claire says, "Let us hope that Princess Beatriz is unharmed!"

Again, Bora calms us by saying, "I am sure Helen will be assessing the situation in their car and will do her best for them all. Until we are out of this situation, we have to keep level-headed and try to think out what our best hope of staying alive is. Panic will only slow us down and cause errors."

"We have no tracking device on this vehicle," Pete says.

"Oh, do not ever underestimate the British Secret Service. All these vehicles used by diplomats and the Secret Service are fitted with tracking devices, as standard, as are all the police cars and emergency vehicles."

We are relieved and Bora continues, "The trick is to show fear to them when they look at you but inwardly be completely calm and be extra vigilant and look out for opportunities."

"Opportunities?" I question Bora.

"To escape, Lucy," he concludes, "every spy worth their salt has, I believe, a duty to escape from their enemies. I find that taking a very deep breath in through the nose and then slowly releasing it through the mouth helps tremendously to calm the body down. Works every time."

All of us immediately take this sound advice.

Immediately, we all visibly relax. Try this exercise whenever you feel stressed or worried; it helps, believe me.

Both cars are closely following each other and we race across London and end up going through Brixton and Thornton Heath and then towards Croydon. The cars keep to the speed limit but only when they are near traffic speed traps; otherwise we are travelling very smoothly and very fast.

"Why Croydon?" Bora asks.

"What does Croydon have that nowhere else near has?" Pete asks.

Claire thinks for ages and then says,

"Dad says that in the War it used to have an airport. Oh, my god. Is that it? Are they intending to take Professor and Princess Mendoza back on a plane to North Kortana?"

"Possibly," Bora says. He could have been more honest and said "probably", but he did not wish to cause us alarm and privately he was already working out ways to help us when we arrived at the airport. As soon as we were on the outskirts of Brixton, he knew where we were heading.

We then pull up in what used to be a very popular airport years ago: Croydon Airport.

Helen, in her car, and travelling with Princess Beatriz and the Professor, is very keen to ensure that those in her care remain safe and alive.

She does, however, have no qualms about her own safety in carrying out her duties as an MI6 Officer, trained in the Highlands of Scotland and the Brecon Beacons, a small mountain range in Wales, and now working for the whole of the UK.

Her wonderful training now kicks in and she swallows hard, almost biting her lip with the adrenaline quickly flooding her arteries. She is trained for action and, if necessary, sacrifice…She takes off her high heels.

As the car pulls to a halt, she throws herself out of the car as she has seen a large old aeroplane taxiing on the single runway that she has quickly deduced will be used by the North Kortanese to fly the Professor and his daughter back to North Kortana.

The plane is on the runway or what used to be the runway many years ago. The runway still has most of its concrete completely intact but there are many weeds and things growing out of it and it looks like it has seen better days. The North Kortanese have obviously managed to land this plane here so presumably take off is also quite possible.

The plane's engines are running so there is very little time to do anything. The pilot then is already on board.

Helen was, at school, praised for her quick thinking and she now has the embryo of a plan.

Bora and Rob, Pete, Claire, Giselle, and I are now all forced onto the plane by the two men with the automatic weapons, followed by the Professor and Princess Beatriz. We feel doomed and are all now feeling anything but calm, especially with Helen out of our line of vision.

With Professor Mendoza now on board there is no reason to hang about and the North Kortanese want to leave as soon as possible. The plane steers towards the wide solitary runway and heads off along it, gathering speed as it does so.

Helen has just one chance to stop it taking off and bravely takes that one chance.

She aims her gun at one of the wheels and shoots, forcing the plane to swerve when the first of the two outer tyres bursts with a loud bang. As it swerves the plane slows down. There are now little flaps of rubber tyre everywhere. She knows there is only one more thing left to try before it takes off as it is not guaranteed that another shot will even hit the tyres.

She aims hard and fires at the pilot's glass at the front of the plane as it passes her and then races along the concrete of the runway after it and manages to not only overtake the plane but also to clamber up onto the high front of the plane. She heroically kicks in the remainder of the glass of the cockpit where the pilot is nursing his arm that she has hit with a ricochet from her bullet, more by luck than anything. Although he is hurt and bleeding from his arm, he carries on trying to fly the plane. He is not armed thankfully.

In only stockinged feet, she manages to kick in enough of the remaining glass to then jump inside the cockpit from the outside, but the pilot, desperate to obey his Beloved Leader still continues to fly the plane along the runway and is intent on still going ahead with his take-off. He feels he must get the Professor back to North Kortana at all costs.

He must also be aware that with the glass of the cockpit smashed that he is really not ever going to realistically make it anywhere. The plane is now fast enough to take off and surprisingly, the plane smoothly takes off and gently rises, minus some of its cockpit glass that drops off and will now remain earthbound.

Helen now quickly opens the cabin door which the pilot has locked from the inside.

She expertly kicks one of the men holding an automatic weapon on the outside of the door while Bora engages the other man in a massive fight to try to wrestle the automatic weapons from them.

The plane continues to climb but the pilot will now need the oxygen mask that has fallen down from the ceiling due to the terrific fall in air pressure. He cannot reach it, however, with his injured, bleeding arm and steer the plane.

Bora makes progress in overwhelming the man he is fighting but only with help from Pete and Rob, who do their best to hold the man's head down on the floor to assist Bora.

Bora wrestles the automatic weapon out of the man's grasp and now pushes it hard into the man and stares coldly into the man's eyes with an obvious meaning. The man does not want to die so he gives up. Bora hands the automatic weapon to the Professor and shouts, "Shoot to kill if he moves!" The Professor nods. The Professor looks ill.

Above the increasing sounds from the plane, Helen now screams to Bora, after hitting the other man hard in the gut and finally overpowering him,

"I can't fly a plane, can you?"

"At least one of us can then," he replies calmly.

He rushes into the cabin and, without much difficulty, manages to move the wounded pilot, who is in shock now and barely breathing because of the drop in air pressure and the cold air, towards the cabin door, where Claire and Giselle assist him to breathe, by placing an oxygen mask on his face. The pilot is exhausted and will offer little resistance now. Both Claire and Giselle sit on him to be sure that he will not recover.

The plane is going up and looks from the ground like it will fall over such is the straight angle of its steep ascent.

Bora immediately grabs the oxygen mask and covers his own face with it. The clear cold oxygen immediately refreshes him into action. His training kicks in and he breathes deeply in to try to control all of his actions. He then grapples with the controls and skilfully turns the plane into a decline where the overtaxed engines might be able to deal with some sort of a descent, before being asked to complete some sort of a landing. Thick black smoke leaks from the engines.

All on board, even Bora, the new pilot, need to use the oxygen masks that have fallen down and hang in the air. This is because of the changes in air pressures as well as the open cockpit window.

Everyone is cold and shivers now as Bora grapples with the smoking plane.

He knows now that he has to land again on what really is a very poor runway that was officially closed as an airport at ten-twenty p.m. on the twenty-seventh of September 1959, according to a sign that I had read when we arrived here.

The plane is way too fast for a landing so he takes it up again and then, mid-air, slows everything down so he can manoeuvre the plane down again towards Croydon Airport. It is not a new plane and responds sluggishly to Bora's skills as a pilot. The engines are noisy and smoke every single time Bora asks them to perform.

The plane has seen better days.

We can see Box Hill from here so we point it out to Princess Beatriz who is largely oblivious to our danger. She only smiles and shivers now with the cold on board this old plane. Her father throws her a blanket.

The boys tie up the three men with help from Helen who even offers her belt to help them do it.

Bora now comes in for a landing and I think we then all hold our breath.

"Brace yourselves for a heavy landing!" Bora bellows at us all against the many sounds that are now becoming deafening.

The noise hits us more than anything else like a wall of pain.

It was a screeching sound as the one wheel without a tyre scrapes along the concrete runway, causing sparks.

Luckily, nothing catches fire.

Bora manages to get this badly damaged plane to skid all over the wide runway but to land safely.

He then forces the plane into reverse thrust to slow us down.

This is a very noisy operation and the plane's engines struggle to obey. More thick black smoke is seen by all.

Police Officers and SAS (Officers from the Special Air Services) are everywhere as the three men are instantly arrested and driven away in separate cars for questioning.

They are roughly handled.

"And what if I had said that I could not fly a plane? What was Plan B?" Bora teases Helen.

"And what if I had failed to get into the cockpit? Would you have been allowed to live on landing at North Kortana with the Professor and the others?" responded Helen.

"Touché!" Bora said and they then hug each other, more with relief than anything else.

Helen cries now with the pains that her body feels now that the adrenalin is decreasing that once flooded her arteries.

Helen has badly damaged her hip and thigh jumping out of the car so she is taken to Mayday Hospital in Croydon for immediate treatment. Her pelvis is realigned by an osteopath at the hospital; glass is removed from her feet.

We are all checked at the scene by medical personnel who have arrived from Croydon Mayday Hospital in three ambulances. The fire crews from the two fire engines that turned up at the airport having nothing to do are able now to have a laugh and a joke with each other. They enjoy hot tea that they have managed to get their hands on from somewhere.

We were lucky and met Helen, Bora, the Professor and the Princess again but it was to be much later on and had to be done in complete secrecy because they were living somewhere in the UK in a safe house as asylum seekers There was no way the North Kortanese could find out where they were living as this would have been the end for the Professor and for the Princess, and depending on where they were located, possibly the end for us as well.

Chapter 15
Buckingham Palace

We have been invited to attend a secret investiture at Buckingham Palace.

We are not permitted to let anyone know about it but Helen Scott is going to be given an award from the Queen of England, Her Majesty, Queen Elizabeth the Second.

Only Helen and all of us will be there.

How cool is that?

We love Helen and really you know it was her bravery that ensured we were not taken against our will to an airport in North Kortana. We would never have returned.

It means we will be given cream cakes and cream teas and Helen will be given the Victoria Cross for exceptional bravery. This is an award that is seldom given.

When it is awarded, it is given for 'most conspicuous bravery, or some daring or pre-eminent act of valour or self-sacrifice, or extreme devotion to duty'.

We cried out aloud with pride and with joy when we were told about this just two days ago.

Helen had not only damaged her thigh but had also broken her ankle either deliberately jumping out of the moving car or when kicking in the glass of the pilot's cockpit to obtain entry into the rising plane. In so doing she risked her life to try to save ours and the Professor's and the Princess Beatriz's life.

Monaie and her dad are also invited, in recognition of their unselfish actions in agreeing to look after the Professor's daughter after her arrival.

No one else, not even the British Press, will be permitted to attend so we feel very honoured indeed.

Monaie is wearing a mauve silk dress and her hair is full of ringlets. Giselle is also wearing a dress that flows long and beautiful around her. Claire looks great in a trouser suit made of linen and coloured rose petal red. When I see just how beautiful both Giselle and Claire really are I can feel my emotions stinging my eyes.

I am looking much older in a beautiful dress paid for by Mum in a shade of light green. I have matching earrings and platform shoes.

Her Majesty has agreed that, exceptionally, we may travel to Buckingham Palace in the blue horse truck and we are moments away from being given permission to enter. The Household Cavalry check out our passes and allow us to enter.

Monaie's dad is wearing a top hat and tailcoat and looks very handsome.

After we are taken in, we wait patiently in a beautiful reception area and suddenly we are confronted by a vision of beauty.

It is Helen looking radiant in a Versace Dress and we feel honoured to share her moment with Her Majesty, who arrives after we have all sat down. Helen has recovered from her injuries. The Queen is wearing a light blue hat and a matching dress with pearls. She is smiling sweetly at all of us, especially at Monaie.

The Queen is, as ever, totally wonderful and appears to be more lovely in real life than the television shows her to be; truly we are blessed with a very elegant and sweet looking Monarch.

Trust me.

Here is a photo taken of Her Majesty, the Queen, on that very day in the grounds of Buckingham Palace.

Her Majesty pins the award on Helen and we are then permitted to applaud.

Senior Officers from MI5 and MI6 and from the SAS take their seats behind us to witness the event and to honour Helen but we have been told not to look at any of them. Not even once.

Just at that moment three armed senior police officers arrive.

They bring in Professor Sebastian Mendoza and Princess Beatriz Mendoza, who has been permitted to dress as a real princess and proudly displays the royal colours of Peru and her small crown.

It is the best day of our lives.

The boys look handsome as well in proper gents' suits and bow ties.

Helen can only stay for a short time but tells us that she will see us soon because the Prime Minister of the day, has directed her to take us out Tuesday for a special treat for helping the UK to learn so much more about North Kortana.

What a RED-LETTER DAY it is going to be.

I can hardly wait.

Chapter 16
Africa on the Thames

Tuesday has taken ages to finally arrive.

'The time is short but the waiting is long' as T.S. Eliot, the poet and writer once wrote. I remember this quotation because Mum often quotes this to me, especially when I am being impatient.

Helen is waiting as we arrive in a paid-for, chauffeur-driven, black MI6 car.

She is wearing blue denim jeans and a smart cream blouse and greets us at Shakespeare's Globe Theatre on the South Bank, adjacent to the River Thames. Do try to visit the Globe Theatre as it is a reproduction of the theatre that William Shakespeare, our most famous playwright, performed his plays in. It even has areas where you can stand like they used to in the seventeenth century.

We have been permitted one more time to see Princess Beatriz and her father, Professor Sebastian Mendoza, and we rush up to first Helen and then Princess Beatriz and then her father, swamping them all with heartfelt kisses and hugs.

We are overjoyed to see Princess Beatriz but sad that this will be possibly the last time that we can see her.

There are at least three armed MI6 officers and Helen on the riverside path to ensure nothing goes wrong. We have no fear any more after what we have been through together.

Rob says, "We have all been through a lot and we have all developed as a result."

Helen agrees and adds, "And I have watched you all grow in confidence as young people. You have all exceeded my expectations."

Claire and Giselle and I take Princess Beatriz to the side of the path and we await our treat. Monaie is with us and her dad and Rob, Giselle, Claire, Pete, Princess Beatriz, and the Professor.

The treat quietly arrives on the water and we are immediately pleased with it.

"A real African canoe with six men and six women to paddle it for us! How great is that?" Pete shouts.

As it nears us, we see that it is a very large and very long canoe.

The President of South Africa has presented this canoe to the UK as a token of improved relations since Nelson Mandela had helped the Africans obtain freedom and we are honoured by being the first to take it out. The Prime Minister of the day had thought that we had deserved it as a reward for our efforts in helping the UK find out more about North Kortana, thereby helping keep the peace in the world.

The canoe is made with the finest hard wood trees in Africa and is luxuriously covered in fake leopard skins and soft furnishings and has a bar and restaurant and even toilets inside as well as cover in the event of rain. It is beautiful to look at and must be at least six metres long with prominent carvings of lions and hippopotamuses. It is a spectacular work of art and has been carefully hand-carved to perfection.

We spend about three hours on the River Thames being paddled at various speeds and even eat a glorious lunch on board. The lunch comprises seafoods from all over Africa and is totally wonderful. The lobster is divine.

Helen Scott and her three companions from MI6 stay on board the canoe for our protection. They are relaxed and seem to be enjoying themselves in what is for them a day off in some respects. They all are, nonetheless, working as their radio mikes show which they each have attached to their ears. They can speak with each other and also with their bosses at MI6.

We see so many sights including the London Eye, which look very imposing from the river, and St Paul's Cathedral and even paddle right along the side of the Houses of

Parliament and can see Big Ben and look up at all the bridges that cross over the River Thames in London. My favourite bridge that we visit is Tower Bridge, which our guide tells us opens for larger ships passing through.

Those men and women who are rowing us in this beautiful vessel have been amazing and have slowed down if we have asked and have shown us also just how fast this large canoe can travel when they row faster.

Giselle stretches out in her seat and declares, "We are so lucky to have such a peaceful day after that awful business at Croydon Airport."

It is a very sunny day in London and we feel blessed to have this time together in peace and happiness.

Pete says, "Finally, we can put all our troubles behind us and enjoy being on the water. The Thames is an incredible place to be during summer and we have been so fortunate to have been offered this canoe, which is so well built and crafted by our friends from South Africa."

Rob has been encouraged to try and learn how to row but the oars are too heavy for him to even lift out of the water. The men and the women rowing smile sweetly at him and are good at responding to all of his and Pete's many questions.

Rob tells us all, "I definitely will learn to row after seeing how great it is."

Monaie has been very relaxed and has for most of the time been sitting between the Princess and her father, the Professor.

Monaie's dad blows smoke rings which lazily drift out over the water and take ages to dissipate in the London sky. Monaie has been very happy taking in all the sights and sounds of what is a very busy river. Many boats containing tourists swiftly pass us on our side of the river.

Completely out of the blue, Monaie asks, "Dad, can you make us a canoe as big and as strong as this one?"

"When would you like it by?"

"By tomorrow morning please Dad."

Monaie's dad replies, "I have to be honest with you, Monaie, that this is an impossible request. I may be able to make a small craft that you can take onto the local village pond at Grove House but that is all I can offer."

We all laugh and even Monaie thinks that his reply is amusing. There is no doubt whatsoever that the Princess and all of us are having a peaceful day on the River Thames.

Having now digested fully the lunch, we are then offered a choice of one final journey to wherever we wish to go to on the River Thames.

We all agree that Princess Mendoza may make this choice and she says, without any hesitation whatsoever, "Please may we place the canoe once again alongside the Houses of Parliament. They are so lovely to look at, especially with the beautiful stonework and stone carvings. The stonework looks to me like the colour of parchment."

The male and female rowers gently turn us around and then glide us again gently towards the seat of government that, a very long time ago, Mr Guido Fawkes tried to blow up and failed. I am so pleased that he failed.

Many call the Houses of Parliament and the House of Lords that make up this wonderful building **The Palace of Westminster.**

I think we deserve this final treat. I think it fitting that the Princess has chosen to revisit a Palace.

What do you think?

Chapter 17
A Brush with Death

Princess Beatriz now has to time to relax. It is certainly true that it has been a very peaceful and enjoyable day and all of us have enjoyed the views.

The Princess watches a small, black speedboat pass near the canoe. This speedboat then comes to a halt near the canoe, approximately one hundred yards away.

Giselle now sits down next to Princess Beatriz on the outer seats near the rowers and they talk about life.

"You must have felt frightened coming all that way in the submarine to England, did you not?"

"Yes, Giselle," responds Princess Beatriz, "but when you need to help your father who is ill, you have to find strength and courage and just do it."

"I suppose so," says Giselle, "but even so, you have done so well to come here, on your own, in a sense."

"The worst part of it was the incessant sounds of the nuclear engine, inside the submarine. It really grated on my nerves. That and my ears popping all the time."

Giselle, at that very moment, stands up to brush her hair, leaning slightly to her left side, and as she does so, she suddenly notices ripples in the brown water of the Thames. These ripples become larger and more noticeable.

Within seconds, someone in a frog suit surfaces and grabs the back of Princess Beatriz and begins to drag her backwards into the water.

Instinctively, Giselle knows who it is and screams at the top of her voice:

"Help! Hye Booh is here! The Princess is being taken!"

Helen immediately makes her entrance and just manages to grab the disappearing legs of the Princess. She holds on to her legs as hard as she can. The struggle leaves the Princess gasping for air as she is submerged now, except for her legs.

The fight for the Princess lasts only seconds but seems to take forever. Taking a risk, Helen now fires her gun at where she believes Hye Booh's head is, to kill her before she can drown the Princess. One zipping shot through the water is all it takes and the Princess is completely freed of Hye Booh's vice-like grip. She has escaped death from drowning by seconds.

The small, black speedboat now makes its way towards where we are and the four MI6 agents continuously fire into the water and then at the speedboat.

Moments later, we see what we believe to be Hye Booh clambering aboard the speedboat and the speedboat's engine is started up and off they go towards Tower Bridge. Although only a small craft, the speed it reaches is phenomenal.

Helen is on her radio mic and shouts amid the noise of the speedboat's engine:

"Suspects have fled scene towards Tower Bridge in a small, black speedboat. The Princess is safe and well."

Helen assures us all that it is unlikely any further attacks will now take place and we all agree that, in view of the fact that Princess Beatriz is recovering well from her recent drama, we shall continue with our plan to pay a quick visit to see the Houses of Parliament in the canoe before returning home.

A small jet crosses the sky above us and Helen informs:

"This is the Royal Air Force, what we call the RAF. They will seek and destroy the speedboat. Have no fear now as we are very well protected. The North Kortanese seem hellbent on punishing the Professor by either kidnapping or drowning his daughter. We must all take greater care from now on."

The Princess has been given a change of clothes by the crew of the canoe and now, believe it or not, is surprisingly well and has even managed to laugh at Monaie's dad who tells us all the story of how he spent a night at sea in a small rowing boat without any oars until he was rescued by his dad the next day. With Monaie's dad, we are never one hundred per cent sure if he is telling the truth or spinning a pirate's yarn.

Monaie's dad concludes his tale and then blows smoke rings that somehow float lazily up towards the lower windows of the Houses of Parliament.

What next? I think and just as I think this, a smoke ring lands on the Princess' wet hair and we all laugh together, feeling relieved that we are safe now from danger. The Princess has kept her cool in what was a very dangerous situation.

We love being in this large canoe and that is why we have stayed in it. Why should we do exactly what the North Kortanese want us to do?

How cool are we to defy them?

Just then, we hear a loud explosion in the direction of Tower Bridge and feel shocked to think that finally Hye Booh has been destroyed along with the small, black speedboat. The RAF have worked their magic.

Thank god for that, we all think.

Can you blame us for thinking this?

Chapter 18
Gladius Mini 100M

Steadily, we are being rowed alongside the Houses of Parliament. They look so majestic from our vantage point onboard the canoe.

It all looks so peaceful and so grand. Monaie's dad also loves the architecture of this building.

Helen's trained ears suddenly pick up zipping sounds in the water near our canoe.

We all have heard six pinging sounds.

PING! PING! PING! PING! PING! PING!

Immediately, we see one of the rowers clutching his shin as blood spurts out of it. The rower looks pale and in great pain but surprisingly she does not scream out. One of her fellow rowers tries to stem the blood flow. Helen now deduces what has fired these mini-missiles.

Helen then is immediately on to her radio to calmly tell MI6, "The North Kortanese are using a Gladius Mini 100M that they have attached a small weapon to in order to try to make holes in the canoe to sink it. Need immediate air assistance and Thames Water Police. The MPU will need to be apprised of the situation."

Apparently the MPU stands for the Maritime Policing Unit who are responsible for policing the Thames.

She turns to us all and then says, "Try not to worry too much but those North Kortanese are using what is known as a Gladius Mini 100M Underwater Drone modified to fire missiles at us to sink us. I have asked for immediate help from my bosses, so try to keep calm and stay still in the canoe as we are sinking."

The canoe, as we soon realise, is now taking on lots of water. Put another way, we are sinking in what is regarded as one of the deepest stretches of the River Thames in a large canoe that we all thought was unsinkable.

Some of the rowers are bailing out water from the canoe's floor but it is a never-ending task. Moments ago, we felt so happy gazing at the beautiful yellow stonework of the Houses of Parliament; now we are all extremely worried. Even though Helen and her three colleagues from MI6 are armed with guns, these guns are useless when someone is operating this Gladius Mini 100M Underwater Drone remotely from somewhere on dry land. Using binoculars, Helen scours the windows of the building, searching frantically for the person remotely controlling the Gladius, invisible to us.

Helen explains that the underwater drone used by the North Kortanese is "only the size of a turtle but is effective unless MI6 can locate it and destroy it". Apparently, they can fit inside a backpack, Helen tells me.

Suddenly, we spot a frogman in the water and just as Helen is about to shoot and kill him, a voice we know is heard:

"It is I, Bora. Do not shoot me!"

Helen shouts at him, "Bora, there is a Gladius Mini Underwater Drone in the area that is armed. Take great care."

Bora responds, "My dear Helen, I am fully aware that we have an unexpected visitor in the water. I have already located it and managed to attach a tracker to it as it sped past me to fire at your canoe. Tell Monaie's dad that they will be rescued from the sinking canoe but they must remain calm. Monaie will be first, followed by Lucy, then Claire, Giselle, Pete and Rob and finally by Monaie's dad. There will be no time to rescue the rowers or yourselves, so you will need to swim to the shoreline where there is some sort of small beach. Are you clear?"

"Totally understood, Bora, but just how will they be saved?"

"Helen, when in doubt, always look upwards to the sky!" Bora says with a great laugh.

On looking up, she sees, and now we see also, two red helicopters arriving high in the skies above Westminster Bridge. Their combined noise echoes on the water, as well as onto the Houses of Parliament and is becoming louder by the second. Some staff working at the building now look out of the windows.

Soon this sound becomes unbearably loud and the water on the Thames that was earlier still, now becomes stirred up and is spraying into our faces with the forces from the helicopters' blades.

"I have tracked the Gladius Mini 100M to just over the other side of your canoe, which means to me that it is returning again to fire some more of its high-velocity bullets into your canoe. You will soon sink. We have no time, so will begin taking our friends from the canoe now."

Helen rushes over just as the first of the hoists arrives above us, being dropped by the first red helicopter. She quickly places Monaie's dad and Monaie on his lap into the winch and they are then winched to the shoreline while the other helicopter nosedives down towards our canoe.

Helen then places us all one by one into the winches while the two helicopters take it in turns to carry us all to the shore.

Bora then screams at Helen, "Prepare for a massive explosion now, they are safely away!"

MI6 have asked the Royal Navy to send a C-Enduro Underwater Sea Drone up the Thames from its base in Richmond, Surrey. The Gladius Mini 100M is no match for the C-Enduro. Meanwhile, the Thames Water Police are desperately trying to trace from where the signals are coming that are operating the North Kortanese drone. The Maritime Support Unit (the MSU) have already granted permission to MI6 to fire a missile under the Thames.

The C-Enduro rapidly picks up Bora's planted tracking device, then confidently sends out its own underwater missile towards the much smaller Gladius. There is a zero chance of failure.

BANG! The inferior Gladius is smashed to smithereens out of the water and parts of its red outer casing are strewn across the Thames. Thick smoke rises, then very quickly disappears over the water.

Helen shouts at Bora, "Well done, Bora! Well done!"

We all clap him as he surfaces near where we have been carefully placed by the brave men and women crew on the two helicopters. Thankfully, the rest of the canoe's crew as well as Helen have all swam to safety on the small beach area under Westminster Bridge, under the watchful eye of the MPU (the Maritime Policing Unit).

Sadly the wonderful canoe has sunk and is no longer visible on the water.

Bora still makes us laugh when we again see him in his waterproof frogman's outfit. Monaie's dad says, "You really are a very remarkable man, Bora."

The London Police now guard us all with their lives as we are now still inside the perimeters of Westminster.

Bora merely replies, "Really, it was nothing. You are all lucky that it was my idea to go for a swim today in the Thames and just was lucky enough to meet you all and help rescue you."

We laugh at his humour.

You and I know very differently of course, don't we?

How cool is Bora?

Monaie hugs Princess Beatriz and then we all do.

Claire is in tears, as I am, with the emotion of it all. Even Rob and Pete look like they have shed a tear or two as we all say goodbye, perhaps for the last time to Princess Beatriz and her father.

We then say a very tearful goodbye to Helen whose bravery has, in the past, really saved our lives.

As a last surprise, Bora is permitted to come out of his Land Rover, where he has been drying off, and hugs us all one by one before Professor Mendoza and Princess Beatriz leave for their safe house somewhere in the UK.

Now it is that Giselle cries many tears as she is forced to confront the idea that she will not see Bora again. They have a special bond between them that will never be broken, I believe.

For sure without Bora, none of us, not even Helen, would have made it back from the Croydon skies on that eventful night. None of us would have survived the attempt to sink us on the Thames. Helen has assured us that he will be secretly rewarded by his own people.

Before we say our final farewell, it is no accident then that we all say with one voice,

"Thank you, Bora and Helen, for saving our lives!"

In the excitement of it all Monaie shouts loudly, "Yes!"

And once again we all laugh and this time Monaie joins in.

As Shakespeare writes in his wonderful play 'Romeo and Juliet', "parting is such sweet sorrow".

How sad to say goodbye to those we care about?

I think definitely that some of the sadness on earth is actually very beautiful to experience. How would any of us know the depth of joy without first knowing the depth of sorrow?

How cool is the sadness of parting from those we care about?

What do you think?

Chapter 19
We All Take a Massive Risk

It was really all of our faults, not just Bora's, nor even Helen's; all of us were to blame for agreeing to meet up one more time with Princess Beatriz and Professor Mendoza.

What were we thinking?

After nearly being taken back in the plane to North Kortana, then nearly being drowned in the River Thames, what were we thinking to agree to see the Princess and her father again, knowing the huge risks we are running?

The original idea came from Princess Beatriz and I have to say only Giselle raised any concerns. Even Monaie's dad, in between puffing smoke rings with his favourite pipe, agreed that, inside the warmth of his lovely home, inside the peace and tranquillity of Sloping Meadow, it seemed like a good idea.

"I think it will be okay especially as both Bora and Helen Scott will be there watching you all and after some three months it will do you all good, at half term, to travel to London Town and see the Princess and her father, the Professor again."

After lunch at Monaie's, we all walked through Sloping Meadow to clear our heads, digest our food and talk.

Monaie told us all in no uncertain way that, "We just have to see Princess Beatriz again. We all care about her and her father, so please can we all agree and go?"

If only it was as simple as that. Monaie had no idea of the great risks we were taking.

Giselle, brushing her beautiful hair back across her face said, "You know, I just want us all to be safe. That is all.

Meeting the Princess and her father, Professor Mendoza, means we shall be taking a massive risk and on balance, I am opposed to the idea."

Rob chipped in, "Giselle, personally I am not frightened of anything or anyone and neither should any of you be, especially with Bora and Helen Scott with us."

Pete, ever cautious, responded with, "Even with their protection, remember the North Kortanese will kill us all if they catch us and will not be interested in taking Professor Mendoza alive since he has by now largely told the UK all he knows about their Nuclear Bombs and rockets etc. The North Kortanese will want their revenge on us all for being complicit in the betrayal of their Nuclear War secrets. They will have no mercy on any of us. They nearly hijacked us all to North Kortana and then tried to drown us on the River Thames in that massive canoe that sunk, or have you all forgotten? "

I then spoke. "Look, I know I am younger than some of you here but I say fear nothing and nobody. That's what Mum always says. Fear nothing and no one. There is a risk that we will be followed and possibly caught by the North Kortanese but all life itself carries risk and you know what, I think we should be prepared to take that risk and live our lives as we would like to, in spite of the risk of harm from others, otherwise we shall do nothing. There is risk everywhere but more importantly there is life everywhere and we need to live and enjoy living without fear."

Pete then said, "You are my sister, and I have to make sure that you are safe as far as I can but, having said that, I am of the same opinion as you, Lucy, that we should meet the Mendozas for one last time in London. Come Hell or High Water! Lucy's right, we should fear nothing."

Rob replied, "I agree."

Monaie said, "So do I."

Giselle then said, "This is against my better judgment but, with reluctance, I now agree. I shall go with the majority vote. I now like Bora a lot and would like to see him again and, of course, I would rather like to see the others as well."

Giselle blushed and now looked even more beautiful than she did a moment ago.

In fairness to her we all knew that she had a special bond with Bora and not one of us teased her about it either. That is the truth.

Claire shrugged her shoulders and said, "Is it not better to live our lives as we wish rather than how some other country's thugs want us to live? I say let us go and meet any danger with courage."

I then recap, "Let it be said then that we all have agreed that we should travel to London Town and meet the Mendozas for one last time to see how they are and to share some fun time with them before this half term is over. And, remember, as far as we know, Hye Booh is dead."

We agreed that we would all travel together to Kershalton Station the next morning at eleven a.m. and travel to Clapham Junction before going to the Southbank to where we are heading.

It was October twenty fourth as we headed back past the copper-coloured beech hedges near Monaie's home and made our way towards our homes. Monaie waved us goodbye just as the light was going and the night was closing in on the very beautiful Sloping Meadow.

We then all promised that we would collect Monaie at ten minutes to eleven the following morning and then all would pick up the train to London Town.

That night I had great trouble sleeping and I am sure that it was because I was anxious about just what we have agreed to do the very next morning,

Will we live to regret what we have all decided upon? Who knows?

Chapter 20
An Eye for an Eye

That Tuesday was cold and it was raining a persistent drizzle. A fine, cold drizzle of rain. Grey London rain. We had all wrapped up but even then the wind punished our faces with its blast of cold, wet air. Leaves, many of which were still green, were made airborne by the winds that were shaking the trees with vengeance.

Monaie looked lovely in her warm boots and a long black coat that covered her knees. She looked the warmest out of all of us. Her dad had recently bought her the coat and it really was splendid.

Giselle started a bit of an argument by stating that in her opinion women should travel in train compartments on their own so that men would not bother them.

Rob said, "If a man wanted to get into a compartment with the women he surely would so there is no point in women traveling alone."

Claire felt that it is better to keep compartments on public transport mixed with both men and women and that this would help everyone get on better and perhaps even feel safer.

Monaie and I stayed out of the argument as we did not really understand it all and, in any event, we soon arrived at Clapham Junction where we changed and made our way to platform ten for Waterloo.

At Waterloo we made our way right to the back of the station and then followed the signs to the left.

Can any of you guys guess where we are going? The clue is in the chapter title.

Yes, it is the **London Eye**. I have never been on it so I am very excited about this.

We are to meet Professor Mendoza and Princess Beatriz at the London Eye. Once there, we shall meet Helen Scott and much later, hopefully Bora.

Walking from Waterloo Station it seemed to take us quite a while to walk past Festival Hall but soon we are confronted by an amazing feat of engineering, as Monaie's dad calls it. The London Eye is certainly very impressive.

Here is Pete's photo of the London Eye from our approach from along the South Bank just moments before we board. The River Thames is adjacent to the London Eye.

Please excuse the poor light but it was autumn and it was raining.

MI6 had already booked and paid for all the tickets on line
so we merely lined up and almost went on to our pod (that's

what you travel in) immediately. Just as we did, we met Helen Scott, casually dressed in denim skirt and denim jacket and with her we saw, with joy written on their faces, Princess Beatriz and Professor Mendoza, her father.

The pod was ready to leave. The London Eye is organised and run by British Airways in the same professional way that they run their Airline so you 'board' this wonderful feat of engineering rather than just walk into it. The pod doors were almost shutting when in came a woman in a mad rush.

We all thought it strange but as the pod begins to rise from the ground into its slow circular path upwards we notice that, when she finally turns to face us, the woman's face is familiar. This is the face we can make out in the reflection of the pod's windows. She is panting from the effort of running to reach us before we ascended.

To our horror it is Hye Booh. The North Kortanese Spy.

She has not been killed by the RAF! The speedboat was destroyed and bodies were found but not hers apparently. Not hers!

This time she is determined to exact revenge for the betrayal of her country's nuclear secrets by the Professor and by any friends assisting him.

She now has no qualms about killing us all.

Her intention is etched clearly onto her face.

Her trained hands are clenching in anticipation of immediate use.

For the second time in our lives together our hearts are in our mouths.

We all stare at her, unable to move for fear, and then we realise that she carries a gun in her hand. It is an automatic weapon. Just then we feel the pod rising to quite a height now but as we do we hear a clunk underneath the pod and think nothing of it, until later.

"**Professor.** A very good day to you and to your royal daughter and to her new-found friends. Fancy travelling on the London Eye and even in the same pod as me. What a marvellous co-incidence, don't you think so, Professor?"

The Professor stays very quiet, as does his daughter, Princess Mendoza. The Professor, I notice, is now shaking.

Hye Booh holds the gun towards us all and says, more to Helen than to anyone else, in clear English:

"One by one you all will die now... and no one this time can help you. I have placed a silencer on the end of my gun so no one outside this pod will even know what I have achieved as no one will hear the sounds of the gun being used to kill you all. One by one you will be eradicated in revenge for the Professor's betrayal of my country, North Kortana, and I, Hye Booh, shall walk out at the end of the flight a free woman and a happy woman. When one considers the level of the betrayal I think you may agree, if you were impartial, that death is a small price to pay for such a catastrophic betrayal of North Kortana."

Largely due to her size and the wider angle that she was able to view because of it, Monaie was the only one who could see just who was desperately trying to climb up the taught strong wire that linked and secured our pod to the rest of the circular London Eye.

It was Bora.

Only Monaie knew this and, thank god, she kept it to herself.

Bora struggled for ages sliding along the tight steel wires with his gloved hands before he could climb above the pod we were in and then lower himself over the front side of our pod and he then indicated to Monaie to open the emergency doors and override the controls. He kept pretending with his free hand to push something to show her what to do and what to press.

Monaie understood immediately and so moved forward and she bravely pressed the only large red button that she thought could achieve this.

In a flash the doors swept open to both sides and in came a rush of cold October air followed closely by Bora with his fists flying; knowing so well that our very lives depend on his actions now.

Helen dives across the floor now and between them they are wrestling what really is North Kortana's number one spy in the United Kingdom.

Helen then receives a very forceful kick from Hye Booh into the middle of her face and she falls down in great agony. Blood begins to drip from Helen's injured face to the floor of the ascending pod. We are very anxious now. Claire begins to sob quietly to herself. Helen has had her nose broken by the awful Hye Booh's kick. Even I can guess that by the cracking sound of poor Helen's nose.

As hard as Bora tries, Hye Booh will not release her automatic weapon and in anger has started firing the gun at the ceiling to frighten Bora away from her. Glass falls from the ceiling when the bullets hit it and the noise of the falling glass makes our ears hurt. We crouch down now together while bits of the ceiling and bits of glass cascade on our heads.

We are all terrified for our lives.

We are very much aware now of just how high we actually are on this London Eye. The winds whistle into the pod now.

Our mouths have all dried up in fear.

Rain also begins to drip into the pod through the broken ceiling glass of the pod and a shiver descends down our bodies as we try to come to terms with what is going on in front of us. We feel at once powerless and fearful for all of our lives.

The temperature drops now as we fear death.

To face death is a terribly cold feeling.

Bora valiantly holds onto Hye Booh's wrist gripping the gun and she keeps trying to turn the gun inwards and onto him.

Suddenly, Hye Booh is free from Bora, who lies on the floor looking defeated.

Hye's look makes it abundantly clear to us all that she now will begin to shoot us all, one by one, with her weapon. She stands firmly with her legs apart now as she confidently levels her gun to shoot us all. She points first at me.

We all swallow hard and dry to face what we now think is an imminent death.

Bora, still on the floor, who earlier has shown no weapon, then produces a dagger from his shoe area and stabs her hard into her foot and, as she screams at him in agony, she fires at his face and a bullet passes through his shoulder, just missing his retreating face.

Giselle then screams at Hye Booh to assist Bora but is powerless for so many reasons; mostly because Giselle has never been trained to fight spies.

Bora now screams in pain and faints but, as he does so, the wonderful Helen Scott charges at Hye Booh and, ignoring her own pain, gives her a flying scissor kick which is so strong and so powerful that it completely breaks Hye Booh's ribcage and knocks her out of the open pod door straight into the grey River Thames, hundreds of feet below.

Hye Booh now lets out a scream that penetrates the whole of the area where the London Eye sits. It sounds like an animal that has been fatally wounded.

As she falls, she still manages to recall her intensive training to fire a few stray bullets towards the London Eye; none of them hitting their targets.

We all gasp at the strength of the kick that Helen has managed to produce and we gasp with sheer relief that we are now safe from the imminent clutches of death.

Having held our breaths for ages, we now exhale together.

I shout out loud, **"OH MY GOD!"**

Claire, I believe, has now just fainted with the sheer shock of everything.

Bora is unconscious now and lies in a heap on the floor. He needs medical assistance urgently. Giselle somehow finds the emotional strength to overcome her fears and tend to him but is crying now; possibly with relief that our ordeal, at such a height and with the doors of the pod still open, is finally over.

She rips the arm of her sleeve to stem the blood-flow. We all manage to place Bora onto the wooden seating in the middle of the pod.

Far down below, the now severely injured Hye Booh manages to swim for at least three or four minutes in the cold Thames water but the sheer effort of fighting with both Bora and Helen Scott is all too much for her fitness and Helen's scissor kick has badly hurt her. Blood seeps from her injured foot into the dirty water.

She begins to swim in what appears to us to be small, hopeless circles.

The River Thames now carries Hye Booh's red blood on its surface. From above it looks as if she is in a rubber ring of blood.

On her beaten face the pain of defeat now clearly shows. Her face is ghostly white with shock and loss of her body's integrity. Hye Booh's time left on earth is now diminishing fast.

Exhausted and definitely feeling the freezing water and its swirls and swells, she sinks into the icy water before rising one more time holding her hand out of the cold water, still clutching her automatic standard issue weapon and then begins slowly sinking to the very bottom of the unforgiving Thames before any lifeguards or river police can reach her.

She makes her very last action alive to be her breathing in solid water deep into her lungs through her frozen nostrils, as she falls ungraciously from this world into a river of death.

The last sight she now witnesses is the very blackness of the murky Thames water all around her and the last experience of life she feels is the icy coldness of the River Thames. Then she slips unhappily away from this material world into the next…unable at the end to hear anything but a gurgling within her own lungs and inside her stomach. Her heart now stops beating as her spirit leaves her still body.

Her bloated physical body washes up at Blackfriars Bridge area two days later on the sandy shore at low tide.

Within seconds of viewing it, MI6 have secured the find and taken a sample of her DNA and then confirmed that it was Hye Booh, a North Kortanese spy, to the Foreign Office.

Much later on, Bora tells me that she has been unceremoniously buried at sea by being thrown from a helicopter. He tells that they will not allow her to become a heroine to North Kortana, to be visited like a celebrity.

We spend the very next day with Helen visiting Bora at St Bartholomew's Hospital, and even Helen cries real tears when she realises just how brave he has been jumping onto the moving pod at the London Eye. It is such a dangerous thing to do. He is an amazing hero and Giselle has become his number one fan.

Giselle's tears are those of relief, relief that Bora has survived. She genuinely cares about him and admires him. Bora will need care and attention for some time to come but he will survive.

We all shudder to think what might have happened to all of us if he had not risked his life to leap onto our moving pod at the London Eye and if Monaie had not then seen him and read his intentions so well and saved us all. Really, the pair of them have been our heroes but, again, if it had not been for Helen's strong kick none of us would have survived for sure.

When we finally return to Sloping Meadow and, this time, we come with at least three escorts from MI6 to protect us, I cannot tell you how pleased and relieved we are. Monaie hugs her dad and when I finally return to my home from Sloping Meadow and Mum asks, "Did you do anything?" I reply this time with, "Apart from seeing off Hye Booh, North Kortana's number one spy, on the London Eye, not much."

Mum then declares,

"Oh, Lucy, you really do have a wild imagination at times, don't you?"

"Yes, I suppose I do," I respond, smiling to myself.

Mum then tells me, "Lucy, apparently Einstein, one of the most famous scientists that has ever lived on earth, once said, 'Imagination is better than knowledge,' so you are in very good company."

I then reply, "When I am older, I will definitely put all these experiences in life that I have had with my friends and The Sloping Meadow into three little books and try and publish the books but who can I ask to illustrate them; perhaps Giselle, who knows?"

Mum asks me if I would like a toasted cheese sandwich which brings me crashing down to earth and, once I have eaten it, I fall fast asleep on our sofa, dreaming of the girl with a parrot, Princess Beatriz Mendoza, Bora, Helen Scott and Professor Sebastian Mendoza and my dear brother Pete, as well as my friends Rob, Giselle, Claire and the lovely Monaie and her lovely, if still at times intimidating, dad.

Oh and I nearly forgot to add. I also was dreaming of our very special Sloping Meadow and the River Bede, flowing fast like a never-ending procession of humanity.

I am sure also that my dream contains Benjamin the donkey and the elusive dormouse that one day I wish to catch, hopefully, in our beautiful Sloping Meadow.

All of us have had a great summer adventure and survived it.

Now we have also just survived an autumnal adventure with Hye Booh, the North Kortanese spy and lived to tell the tale.

We are survivors.

How cool are we?

THE END OF THE SECOND BOOK OF THE *SLOPING MEADOW* TRILOGY